CLEAN AS A WHISTLE

Slocum eased his tall frame into the swirling river. Able to find his footing in the knee-deep water, he drew in a deep breath. Then he threw his head back to plaster his black hair away from his face with his palms. Something caused him to turn and listen for a new sound above the river's rush. Horses were coming—lots of them.

Fifty feet from his weapons, personal things, and hobbled horses, Slocum swore under his breath as he scrambled over the mossy, round rocks for the shore. The approaching hoofbeats sounded to him like the entire Mexican army was charging up the river valley. A fool and his bathing pleasures would be short-lived if he didn't get his guns . . .

JAKE LOGAN

SLOCUM AND THE APACHE RANSOM

JOVE BOOKS, NEW YORK

SLOCUM AND THE APACHE RANSOM

A Jove Book / published by arrangement with
the author

PRINTING HISTORY
Jove edition / July 1996

The Putnam Berkley World Wide Web site address is
http://www.berkley.com

ISBN: 0-515-11894-X

A JOVE BOOK®
Jove Books are published by The Berkley Publishing Group,
200 Madison Avenue, New York, New York 10016.
JOVE and the "J" design are trademarks
belonging to Jove Publications, Inc.

PRINTED IN THE UNITED STATES OF AMERICA

10 9 8 7 6 5 4 3 2 1

1

April 1886

He eased his tall frame into the swirling river. The cold forced him to suck in his breath as his slim hips settled into the water. Under the clear surface, his bare skin shone like ivory. Small whirlpools were formed downstream by the current knifing around him. There still must be snow melting on the peaks, Slocum decided, as he squatted neck-deep in the Rio Blanco's swift flow.

Then he caught a deep breath and bobbed his head under the surface, to let the river's chill erase the sun's scorching heat from his face. Relief came at last as the water's healing powers began to draw out the fire from his skin. Letting his breath out slowly, he remained squatted on the river's bottom and used his hands to dog-paddle to maintain his position. Finally, his breath long spent, he surfaced into the brilliant sunlight making strong strokes with his arms to reach the shore.

Able at last to find his footing in the knee-deep water, he drew in a deep breath. Then he threw his head back to plaster his black hair away from his face with his palms. Something caused him to turn and listen for a new sound above the river's rush. Horses were coming—lots of them.

Fifty feet from his weapons, personal things, and hobbled

horses, he swore under his breath as he scrambled over the mossy, round rocks for the shore. The approaching hoof-beats sounded to him like the entire Mexican army was charging up the river valley. A fool and his bathing pleasures would be short-lived if he didn't get his guns.

The giant, gnarled cottonwoods and willows chocked the river bottom and obscured his view of the oncoming horses as the drum of their hooves grew closer. He fought his britches on over wet legs. Finally, with a Navy Colt ready in his right hand, he jerked up his clothing and, hat, boots, and saddle under his arm, raced barefooted to his horses. Sharp rocks and thorns stabbed his bare soles as he ran.

The first loose horses swept past between him and the river, quickly followed by many others, all well-bred stock. Gun ready, he dumped his gear on the ground, anxious to see who drove them.

Out of the dust that the horses churned up, he saw a copper face. But the Apache herder quickly ducked down on the far side of his pony and was swept by him in the rush. However, the young warrior's earsplitting ki-yacking war cry was enough for Slocum to know that the boy had warned the whole nation of his presence. Damn, how many were there?

Slocum used a large tree trunk for a shield as he tried to catch sight of another buck. Even as a hard rock of dread formed in the pit of his stomach, he knew one thing. If somehow he managed to survive this afternoon, he would never need another four-leaf clover. In his mindless wandering across Sonora, he'd fallen smack in to the middle of a full-fledged renegade retreat. There was no mistaking the youth's origin; he was Chiricahua. They must have fled their U.S. reservation again. The only reason he could imagine for such haste in loose-herding that many horses was that the military was after them. Either U.S. or Mexican forces, or both, must be close behind. These young bucks were driving good horses they'd probably acquired them in a ranch raid somewhere, and were taking them into the vast folds of the Sierra Madre Mountains.

He glanced aside at his own mounts, a buckskin and bay.

They calmly remained busy grazing with the passing of the herd. Satisfied that the horses and herders was gone, he turned aside to finish his dressing when a sharp voice challenged him, "White man!"

Colt still in his hand, Slocum spun on his heels to frown at the three Apaches on horseback approaching him. They wore black paint on their faces and their headbands were made from black silk, except for the one in the center, who wore a blue bandanna on his head. Each one of them balanced a repeating rifle on his knee. They stopped at a range that made his .31 less than certain. In in instant, he could cut down two of them, but the third one would be shooting back before his bullet reached him.

"What are you doing here?" the leader demanded.

"I don't have to report—" Slocum corraled his anger. "I'm headed for Santa Cristo."

"To sell scalps?"

"No!" If they thought he was a scalper of women and children, he intended to set the record straight. There were plenty of border scum selling black hair to the Mexican authorities. But Slocum was not one of those money-thirsty dogs.

"Look my things over." He tossed his head in the direction of his packs. "I'm damn sure not a scalper. Never been one." He still held the Navy in his right hand ready for them to make the next move. "Who are you?"

"Natise."

"The son of Cochise?" As he waited for a reply, Slocum wondered what the threesome were saying about him in their guttural language. He understood Apache, but not at a mumble. Then the hard-faced Natise pushed his horse closer. He squared himself off as if only he and Slocum existed under the rustling cottonwoods.

"Cochise is dead," Natise said.

"A shame. He would have led his people in peace."

"No. He would have done as we have and left San Carlos."

Slocum met the man's cold stare and shook his head in disbelief. "I knew Cochise. He was a man of his word."

"He would never have shared a camp with the cowardly Coyoteros and the stinking Yavapis. They don't even speak Apache!"

Things had certainly changed since Tom Jeffords ran the Chiricahua Reservation out of Apache Pass. When had they shipped these mountain people to that malaria hellhole on the Gila? Anyone with a lick of sense knew the Chiricahuas had little use for most of the western tribes of their nation.

"How long ago did they move your people to San Carlos?" he asked.

"Two years ago."

Slocum chewed on his lower lip. The prickly stubble fringe cut his upper lip as he drew his sharp teeth over his bottom one. What Natise had said put a new light on this outbreak.

"Tom Jeffords. Where is he?" Slocum asked.

"Tucson—he can do nothing." Natise dismissed the notion with a head shake.

"Can't he speak for your people?"

"No one speaks for the Chiricahuas!"

In deep disbelief, Slocum drew a deep breath and indicated Natise. "Then the son of Cochise must speak for them."

"Speak to who? Natan Lupan is gone." Natise made a wide sweep with his left arm to say that General George Crook wasn't in Arizona to hear them. "We should speak to the man who gives out wormy meal and gives us cows so thin we must chew the hide for nourishment? No, we are not beggars like the western tribes. We will die to the last woman and child in these mountains before we will return to such treatment."

"Do you lead these people?" Slocum asked.

"No. They go with who they trust. There are many leaders today."

"Some fine horses went by here," Slocum said.

Natise grinned for the first time, and his bare chest, under the unbuttoned non-com blouse, puffed a little. "No one can steal horses like a Chiricahua."

"No one," Slocum agreed. "I once knew your father.

He gave me a medal of friendship.''

"You knew Jeffords too?"

"Yes, but it has been many years."

Natise pushed his horse in closer. "You have stripes on your back. I remember seeing them."

"Scars," Slocum agreed as he held the Colt's barrel in his left hand, still ready in case they tried anything.

Natise halted the bald-faced horse a few feet from Slocum. "Do the ones who whipped you so hard still walk the land?"

"Only one."

"What do they call the friend of Cochise?" His diamond-black eyes narrowed as if he tried to recall it.

"Slocum."

The chieftain nodded as if digesting the name. "Slo-cum, do not stay in these mountains. It is easy to kill an enemy, but hard to kill a friend. You have been a friend to the Apaches in the past, but now we have no white friends." Natise shifted the rifle balanced on his leg. "Don't ride back through this land. I would hate to see the blood of my father's friend splattered on these rocks."

Without another word, he turned his horse and rode south after the horse herd, long gone from hearing. The other two rode past ignoring Slocum. They set rawhide heels to their ponies, issuing hair raising ki-yis racing after their leader.

When he was alone under the rattling cottonwoods, despite the sun's heat, a cold gust of wind swept over his bare chest as drops of icy sweat from his armpits dripped on his ribs. He would live. Live to see another day. Even view a Mexican sundown, drink some hellfire tequila, and sleep in a bed with a beautiful witch in Santa Cristo.

A small shudder shook his shoulders as he tried to dismiss his close brush with death. He shoved the Colt in his waistband and swept up the long-sleeved shirt. Each button absently slipped in place as he reconsidered his good fortune. Apaches seldom left witnesses alive.

Where was the token that Cochise had given him? Somewhere, if he hadn't lost it. Tom Jeffords lived in Tucson. Slocum recalled the big man. Maybe he would swing up that direction one day and see him, tilt a few glasses, and learn what happened to the treaty that Cochise and Jeffords had struck with Washington. No telling what those civilian fools in charge of Indian policy were thinking about.

He jammed the Colt into the holster and buckled on the belt. Seated on a log, he held up the first sock and shook his head at the hole in the toe. He'd need to find someone to mend it. Then he brushed off the sand and sticks from his sole to roll the sock on. His horses still grazed close by as he drew the boot on his foot. He strained to shove his heel down the vamp and into place. Finally forced to stomp it in place, he stopped to study the vast pine-clad slopes around him. With his nose full of the fresh pine smell, nothing appeared out of place that he could detect as his foot finally slipped into place. The Coffeeville Kansas boot maker was good at his trade, but he'd cut this latest pair a little tight.

He seated himself again and put on the other sock and boot with less effort. Dressed, he shrugged on the vest and went for the horses. Only a fool stayed where he wasn't wanted. Sounded like the Chiricahuas were fragmented into small bands across the Sierra Madres. What had Natise said? Many leaders.

Slocum slipped the curb bit in the buckskin's mouth, speaking to him out loud in the habit of a man alone most of the time. "Buck, we've got that mountain west of here to clear. Hope you and Jimbo got a belly full of this good grass while you had the chance."

He checked around, but only a saucy jay in the branches above shared his company. He unhobbled Buck, then the bay Jimbo, and led the pair to where his saddle was stacked on its end, without telling his horses how close they'd came to becoming war ponies. For a second, he quit the saddling process to consider the steep ponderosa-clad mountains around him. In earlier times, their vastness had been a place where he could let his guard down, even clear his head. Those days were gone.

Slocum jerked up the latigo as he kneed Buck hard to

stop the animal's swelling against the girth. In disgust, he shook his head over the turn of events. There wasn't a place left on this earth for him to escape. Even the Sierra Madres had become a battlefield.

Why didn't politicians stop breaking Indian treaties? Because they were so greedy and they didn't give a damn who got hurt by their mistakes. So the innocent settlers and their families, caught among the raging savages, paid with their lives. Not to mention the Apache squaws and children; Apache men were warriors and death was their lot, as it was for the veteran troopers who took up their tracks.

With the packsaddle on Jimbo, pannier boxes straps slung over the cross bucks, tarped, and then tied down, he swung up on Buck. With tight lips and a head shake of disapproval, he eyed the gurgling, clear Rio Blanco—damn shame to have to leave it.

He booted Buck westward up the mountain. He did look forward to Estrellia Tomas's company in Santa Cristo. As he surveyed the river's twisting valley to the south, there was no sign of Natise nor his horse herd's telltale dust sign. Slocum could recall the mountain *rancheria* of Cochise, swallowed up in the green pinery somewhere, and the pretty young women in the camp who had caught his eye. Gone too.

There was a deep turpentine smell in his nose, and a cool wind hushed through the pines boughs as he reached up for the curled brim of his weatherbeaten Stetson to set it down on his head. Grateful that the Apaches' escape from Arizona was not his personal problem or worry, he set Buck into a long trot.

2

Santa Cristo's church tower shone above the village's high walls in the late afternoon sun. The belfry's 'dobe coating look gilded with gold in the bloody light, and the great bell that had hung for two centuries glinted inside the arched openings as if it was made of the precious silver that the surrounding mountains yielded.

A fortress built by the Spaniards in their long war with the Apaches, it had lasted over two hundred years. Slocum knew despite the white man's attempts to take the land away from the *Indios,* until recently the red man had controlled all of Sonora, as well as the southern half of Arizona and New Mexico territories. Santa Cristo was thought worth fighting for only because of the silver mines. Some politico in Mexico City had decided the state could justify building a walled defense and equipping the fortress with military for the gains that could be drawn from the bowels of the Madres.

As he reined Buck around a fresh rock slide across the trail, he recalled the hostiles' opinion of the Mexican soldier. A sub-chief, Jeru, had told George Crook during the Skull Canyon peace signing, when the Apaches agreed in 1882 to return to the reservation that his warriors saved their bullets for Americans; they could kill the Mexican soldiers with rocks. Slocum recalled how Crook had removed his trademark pith helmet, laughed until tears ran down his face, and been forced to spread his hands on the ground to support himself.

Where was Crook? In Washington? Probably had a powerful desk job—no more desert thorns in the ass for him. He'd beaten the Apaches once, then given the Sioux-Cheyennes hell. Rode a gray mule across Arizona in the last campaign, a wiry tail-wringer that the chief scout, Al Siebling, had found for him. Crook had called the noisy braying critter Apache—appropriately. Where was Al and that carefree squaw-chasing rip Tom Horn? Up in Arizona, he supposed, they no doubt were busy packing mules, raising troops, and recruiting Apache scouts to head south with half the U.S. Army to put an end to this outbreak. Enough fretting about them; they could take care of themselves.

Santa Cristo looked good to him as he rode through the open gates. A young soldier was seated on his butt at the entrance; he did not stir at Slocum's passage. The private's musket lay beside him as he snored with his head resting against the wall.

With Buck in a swinging walk, Slocum grinned to himself about the village's fine guard as he rode up the passageway to the center of the square. At the stock tank beside the well, he dismounted heavily. Jimbo came in beside Buck, and both horses dove their muzzles in the water and began to swallow hard.

"Hands in the air, hombre!" someone ordered.

Peeved at the inconvenience of the man's orders, Slocum turned around. His hands raised shoulder high, he studied the full-faced sergeant who waved an old Walker Colt with authority at him.

"I will take that gun," the noncom said, and leaned forward to relieve him of his revolver.

"What's the charge here?" Slocum asked the full-bellied man with the thick mustache and the billed cap.

"Selling guns to the Apaches. We have been waiting for you for several days, señor."

"You don't even know my name." Slocum looked around for someone to come to his rescue.

"It makes no difference what you call yourself. You answer the description of the man that my captain wants held for selling guns to those red devils."

Slocum spit in the dust. "You have the wrong man. Why would I ride in here if I was friends of the Apaches?"

"Sergeant Gomez!" The boy who'd been asleep at the gate shouted as he came running out of breath, dragging his musket. "Oh, you have him. He tried to slip by me."

"How did he get by you, stupid?" the sergeant demanded.

The soldier drew himself up to attention. "I don't know, my sergeant. Maybe he is a ghost too."

"Maybe you were asleep?"

"Maybe I went to pee and he rode by."

"Next time, Benito, you better hold on to your bladder. You hear me?"

"Oh yes, my sergeant."

"No tricks either, gringo," Gomez warned, waving the great horse pistol around in a threatening manner that only drew a scowl from Slocum.

"May I see that my horses are properly stabled?" Slocum asked, weary of the two clowns and wishing for a few good rocks to finish them off with.

"Ha, where you are going you won't need no horses. When the captain comes, he will probably order you shot at sunrise."

"Good, but these horses are too valuable—"

"Never mind. When I lock you in the calaboose, I will see they are well cared for. I could use such a horse as the buckskin." Gomez gave the horse a greedy appraising look.

"Treat them good, Gomez, or my ghost will haunt you the rest of your miserable life."

"I told you he was a ghost!" Benito said, with a wary shake of his head. "That is how he got by me at the gate."

"Shut up," Gomez said as if considering the threat. "Move, that way," he ordered Slocum, pointing to the east side of the square.

"I can handle him now," the boy said.

"Just the same, I will walk with you over there," Gomez

said. "The captain wants this gringo held until he comes, or off go both our heads."

"I savvy," Benito said, sounding impressed. "What is his name?"

Gomez nudged Slocum in the back with his pistol. "Who are you?"

"Joe Smith," Slocum lied.

"See, Benito, his name is Smith."

"Is that his real name?"

"Is that your real name, gringo?" Gomez asked, reaching ahead to open the thick cell door.

"You want to see my passport?"

"You have one?" Gomez asked.

"In my shirt pocket." Slocum indicated the left one. And at the man's nod, he fished out the bill of sale from the stables in El Paso for the two horses. He handed the folded paper to Gomez.

The noncom cleared his throat with an air of authority and waved the paper open as Benito crowded in close to see it too. The boy pointed excitedly at the top of the page.

"Eagles!" Benito indicated the two birds that framed the stables' name, Offenheimer's Livery. "It must be official, huh? What does it say?"

"His name is Joe Smith, stupid. Can't you read," Gomez said with a displeased look at the private.

"No, I can't read." The boy drew back as if he expected a blow to his ear. "I never went to no school."

"And you will always be a dunce," Gomez said with his newfound superiority.

Slocum kept a straight face as he refolded the receipt and put it back in his pocket. Weary of the pair of fools, he searched around the darkening courtyard for any one to save him from imprisonment as the final sun's rays shone on the bell. Then in surrender, he ducked his head to go under the low doorway and entered the cell. He overheard the private quiz Gomez about a missing key for the lock, before Benito could be hushed by his superior.

"Gringo. My man has orders to shoot you if you try to escape," Gomez warned, his fists wrapped around the bars of the small window in the heavy-timbered door.

Slocum grunted that he had heard the man's threat. The cell was dark save for the small square of sundown coming in the doorway opening when Gomez moved aside. It was a dank filthy-smelling cavern, the only hope the single fleeting patch of daylight shining on the back wall. Slocum dropped to the hard bunk and drew out the two-shot derringer from his pocket. He might have need of it yet. How had he ridden into such a dumb trap? What a mess. He replaced the pocket gun for later usage.

"Private!" Slocum shouted.

"Señor?" a mouselike voice answered beyond the thick door.

"Go find the Señora Estrallia Tomas."

"I can't leave my post."

"Find a messenger. She can testify who I am."

"Why do you want her?"

"She's my sister."

"Oh, señor, surely you must joke. Señora Tomas is not your sister."

"Ask her!" Slocum shouted as he removed his hat and set it on the bunk beside him. Then he dropped his chin in his palms, braced on his knees. Jailed by the bungling military, he could think of a million better places to be than this stinking cell. He'd planned on a good drunk and a rich meal—his stomach complained for the lack of food. For days Estrallia had been on his mind as he rode leisurely across the Sierra Madres. The private knew her, so she still lived in the village. Where was that witch? Yes, Estrallia was a real witch and a doctor too.

"Open the door, you stupid donkey! That man in there did not sell the Apaches any guns!" a commanding woman shouted at the private who whimpered from what sounded like fists being pounded on his head and back.

"Stop!" Benito begged. "Let him out yourself. The door is not locked."

The timber closure creaked under protest as it swung open, and the twilight outlined the woman's hands on hips stance as she blocked the opening. He couldn't see her face in the poor light as he rose to depart his prison.

"Took you long enough," Slocum said, setting the hat on his head and started after her.

She reset the black *reposa* over her head, and without a word turned on her heel as if she expected him to come along. He ignored the babbling boy, and followed her out through the porch and across the darkening square.

"Listen, where are my horses?" he asked, not seeing them in the square.

"They have been stabled," she said, and pushed open the carved front door to her place.

He smelled the spicy food that he recalled she fixed, along with her perfume and musk, which hung in the room. No lamps were lighted. It was dark, but the apartment held the promise of her silky-smooth bare skin atop a bed of feathers.

Slocum thumbed his hat up as she shut the door behind him and sweep off the shawl, then hung it on a peg. Then she turned and hugged him like a hungry bear, pressing her hard breasts into his belly. He kissed the top of her head and rocked her in his arms as she clung to him.

Her arms soon encircled his neck and pulled his face down to her fiery mouth. Her serpentlike quick tongue sought his. His hand explored her back, ribs, and hard butt under the full skirt as he savored her lust and closeness. Her mouth tasted of honey, and her hot tongue entwined with his until he grew dizzy with desire.

Slowly she released his neck and dropped down from her toes until her full five-four height stood close before him. Then out of nowhere, she drove a sledgehammer fist into his solar plexus. "Why did it take you so long to return this time?"

Short of breath, he stumbled back against the door. "I— I—been—busy," he gasped.

"Busy," she snorted in disbelief. "Come along, you aren't hurt. You smell like a goat, and I suppose you have not eaten in days. You are thinner than ever. Don't you ever eat with those other women in your life?" She lighted a lamp and raised it to look him over with a nasal, "Hmm."

A quick toss of her long hair and she set the lamp on the table. "Food first."

"Good," he said, settling into a high-back chair. He surveyed the dishes he had smelled coming inside. He followed her shapely hips as she went for a bottle from the shelf.

"I only have wine," she apologized as she threaded the corkscrew downward.

"That's fine. My, this food looks like enough for an army and smells good too."

"You still say pleasing things." She covered her amusement with her hand.

He stopped fixing his plate and stared at her hard. "You don't look a day older."

"Then if I am so gorgeous, why has it been such a long time since you have been here?"

"Two years?"

"More like three years, hombre." She began to fill his goblet with the red wine.

"I guess I got busy and lost track of time."

She frowned in disbelief at him. "I was shocked when I saw in the stars that you were coming."

"What else did they tell you?" he asked with the large meat-filled tortilla close to his mouth.

"That you might be run over by horses coming here."

"Close enough. I damn near had that happen," he said before biting in the food. She still had the power to see in the future—almost uncanny. Somehow, he had known as he rode this way that she was alive and would welcome him.

"I was afraid that you would be hurt by them."

"Natise let me live to come see you again."

Her olive face paled as she considered his words. "You were with that butcher?"

"I was, let's say, his unwilling prisoner for a few minutes."

"How did you get away?"

"I knew his father Cochise."

"Butchers. Everyone of them. They kill and rape the

people and steal their livestock. I hope they all are killed!
This village is never safe.''

"Stop buying the damn scalps then," he said, busy mop-
ping up the red sauce with a fresh tortilla.

"You know the government buys them. The people here
have no money." She shrugged off his accusations.

"They come here to collect, don't they?"

She barely nodded and, her arms folded, looked the other
way. Slocum refilled his plate. One thing he knew for certain. She never lacked for fire.

"Who is this captain?" he asked.

"Raowel. He is a small hyena who barks a lot. The only
soldiers he has are the donkeys like Gomez who are bum-
blers. When the Apaches want us, they will take this village." She shook her head in disgust, pursing her lips as
she bent over to refill his wineglass.

"Why do you stay here then?"

"Where would I go?" she asked in a small voice.

"Across the border."

"No, these people need my care."

He finished the food, feeling full. Over the rim of the
goblet he considered her; midwife, healer, and fortune
teller. She took her role seriously. Once, long ago, she had
healed a bullet wound in his side. Slocum could recall the
pain he'd felt when bent over in the saddle, roped in by
Tom Horn so he couldn't fall out on the trip over the mountains to this place. She had made him a new man in his
months of convalescence in her home.

He rose to straddle the chair. "Where's the bath for a
goat?"

She laughed aloud and crooked a finger for him to follow
her. As he stepped over the seat, a knock on the door sent
his hand to his empty holster. With no gun, he swore under
his breath as she blocked his way, She caught his arm and
held it as if he had a pistol in his grasp.

"You have no enemies here," she whispered, and in a
swish of the full skirt she went to answer the door.

He would need his Navy back, or the spare gun in his
saddlebag. He listened to the man's voice. Someone needed

her services. Slocum hoped she wasn't being called away to deliver a baby or to treat a sick person. He had other plans of his own for her as he stood back from the light on the table and waited.

She crossed the room to him. "Come," she said. "The Don wishes to speak to you."

"Who?" Slocum asked with a disproving frown.

"Don Miguel Sallisar." She tugged on his sleeve to lead him toward the table.

The other man, with an expensive sombrero in his hands, came closer too. He wore a well-tailored waistcoat and leather pants. This man was no common vaquero, and Slocum figured he had not come for the services of a midwife.

Impatiently she waved for Slocum to come closer.

"Don, this is the man I told you was coming. His name is Slocum."

"Señor." Slocum offered his hand.

Finished shaking, they both sat down at the table as she poured more wine. The Don refused his glass, but she let it sit before him as the two men appraised each other.

"The stories they tell of you are many," the Don said.

"Miguel, all right to call you that?"

"Certainly."

"Good. Every day men tell lies about bravery over liquor at the cantina. What do you want of me?"

"The Apaches are holding his daughter Lucia for ransom," she explained, standing close beside Slocum so he could smell her musk.

"I have paid them once, but they did not return her," Miguel said.

Slocum drummed his index finger on the tabletop. He looked hard at the man. "Maybe she is dead."

"No, Lucia's alive. Last week the Apaches came to trade in a village not twenty miles from here, and she was with them."

"How long has she been gone?"

"Three months. It is killing my wife and my mother. I only have one daughter." He reached in his pocket and put a paper photo on the table. "See what a beauty she is?"

Slocum studied the picture of the girl. Fine clothing, a ripe figure, and proud bearing. Yes, by her appearance, she was the spoiled daughter of a hacienda owner.

"I can pay you well," Miguel said.

"They may have killed her since that day when someone last saw her." Slocum wanted the cards out on the table with this man before he agreed to a thing.

"Two hundred dollars American."

"If I do agree to go look for your daughter, which I have not agreed to yet, you understand the Apaches may want more ransom."

"I don't care, I will pay it. My wife cries day and night for her return."

"Lucia is a lovely girl," Estrallia said. "You will help this poor man?"

"By now she may carry an Apache baby." He wanted the father to know everything before he ever accepted the job.

"I don't care. My house . . ." The Don shook his head with great sadness in his eyes. "My family cannot live without her."

Slocum sunk in the chair. The girl was somewhere in the Sierra Madres in an Apache rancheria. What had Natise warned him? Leave these mountains, he'd said. It was hard to kill a friend, but Apaches no longer had any white friends.

The tired man across the table, with the deep lines of worry in his brow, wanted Slocum to go up there and search for his daughter. Maybe he should simply ride on. The lovely girl in the creased, worn picture was no doubt from a more tender place than an Apache rancheria. Slocum closed his eyes and daydreamed about more peaceful days and times when hard decisions weren't all he made.

Finally filled with newfound resolve, he opened his eyes to look across the table at the Don. He raised his lanky frame up in the chair and put his elbows on the tabletop.

"I can promise you nothing. But I will go look for her."

"*Gracias*, señor." A flood of relief took ten years off the man's face. "Estrallia has told me if anyone—"

Slocum held out his palms to warn the man and slowly shook his head. "I don't tell fortunes, but I don't hold much for anyone's chances of doing this successfully."

"Slocum," she whispered intimately close into his ear. "Your generosity will be rewarded for doing this."

He reached up and patted the side of her smooth face as the weary father drew himself to his feet.

"God be with you, Slocum."

He would need to be, and a million saints as well—*Hard to kill a friend . . . hard.*

3

Sporadic gunshots and a hurrah of voices outside awoke Slocum. He raised up on his elbows, naked atop the bed, and turned his ear toward the noise in the square. Some kind of hellraisers were out there—not raiders. He dug out the oil-smelling Navy Colt from under the pillow; Estrallia had secured the revolver along with his things from the livery while he had taken a bath the night before.

He stretched his tight back muscle as he sat up. Sometime after she had shaved his face and trimmed his hair, the very moment when his hands had affectionately molded her shapely hips, someone had knocked on her door. Hat in hand, the man had asked for her to come and help his poor wife who was in labor. With a quick kiss for Slocum, she had promised to return shortly, then rushed off to deliver the baby.

Now it was past dawn, and she still had not returned. There must have been serious problems with the delivery. He closed his eyes as more gunshots shattered the morning. Damn *pistoleros* would have the sky so shot full of holes it would rain like a sieve for a week. He pulled on his pants, buckled on his gun belt, replacing the Navy into the holster, and went out the back door to relieve himself.

The cool air tingled on his smooth-shaven face as he stood in the shadowy alley emptying his bladder. He could still hear the hellraising sounds in the square out front. They must have just arrived—they sounded like Americans from their scattered shouts. Border riffraff, no doubt.

Finished, he went back inside, found his Stetson, put it on his head, and went out the front door. From the porch he watched a staggering drunk wearing a bowler hat wandering around the square with a pistol in one hand and a brown bottle in the other. Besides the bowler, the man wore the clothing of a Texas cowboy.

He paused and blinked in disbelief at Slocum. Then he squinted at Slocum's approach as if he had found a new threat. Waving his gun hand, the drunk tried to stand up as if to face off with him.

"His bloody gun's empty, lad. Don't kill him," a burly, red-faced man said to Slocum from the arch in front of the cantina. "Good men are hard to find these days."

His thick Scottish brogue matched his Highlander outfit and plaid tam atop a profusion of red hair. Slocum guessed the Scot's age to be near fifty. He was a big man with amble bulk, but his green eyes held a lot of unanswered things that made Slocum draw some caution.

"Good men are getting hard to find, and he's only having fun," the Scot said. "Me name's McVain."

"Slocum," he said, still with a wary eye on the drunk as he passed him.

"Aye, I've heard of you," McVain said, sounding pleased as he used his hand to show the way inside the cantina.

"Your bunch sure cuts a man's sleep short," Slocum said, stopping short of the man in his red plaid kilts with the blanket over his shoulder.

"Come on, I will repay you for the inconvenience," McVain said, and he let Slocum enter the swinging doors first.

A half-dozen sets of hard eyes faceted on him when he entered. The *putas* smiled at him as they lounged on the men's laps. A few of the men's faces looked familiar, but Slocum had no names to attach to them. Some of the hardcases had no doubt been buffalo hunters or connected with the trade as Slocum had been. The last years of the big hunt had brought out lots of men without real names and with their pictures plastered on wanted flyers.

"Lads, this gentleman's name is Slocum," McVain said. "We owe him a drink for disturbing his sleep."

The man's words brought a hurrah of laughter from his gang. With a nod of acknowledgment Slocum then turned to the Mexican bartender and ordered a double shot; McVain asked for the same.

"Lively place, huh?" McVain asked.

"I kind of figured it was a good place to sleep until you all arrived."

"A man only comes to this mangy place for one purpose," McVain said, looking into the smoky mirror on the wall as he raised the glass to his lips and waited for an answer to his statement.

"I'm just riding through," Slocum said.

"They say the Chiricahuas fled the reservation two weeks ago."

"I've heard that."

"How's the gun trade?"

Slocum raised the glass and carefully looked at the clear yellow-tinged liquor. "Someone lied to you. I don't sell guns to Apaches or anyone."

McVain acknowledged the words while still staring into the mirror. "Folks get things mixed up, don't they?"

Slocum downed the rest of the glass. The hot liquor went down his throat like a flash fire and the fumes burned his sinuses close to the point of tears. He slapped the glass on the bar.

"They damn sure do. I don't collect scalps either."

"Ah, lad, you don't approve of me business. I can tell by the very tone of your words. But I ask you, what are we to do? The buffalos all gone, we can't do that no more. Freighters are being run out of business by the damn railroads. I ask, what is an honest man to do?"

"I guess sell tacos on the street corner," Slocum said.

"That's a good one," the Scotsman said, forcing some laughter before he resumed his inquisition.

"I say you have some kind of business in this quaint village that will turn a coin." McVain held up a gold twenty-peso coin that glinted even in the smoky dark canteen light. "I have the money for the next drink."

"No thanks, Mr. McVain. I need to see about some things."

McVain turned to face the room and rested his elbows on the bar. "You there, girl, get off his lap. Get over here." He pointed at the doe-eyed whore and crooked his finger for her to come.

The man whose lap she sat upon laughed out loud as if he was expecting something to happen. Uncertain, she rose. The man gave her a shove from behind, and she half stumbled toward McVain, stopping a few feet short.

"Take off your clothes," McVain said, a look of mischief written on his lips. "Go ahead, girl, we've all seen your bare ass before."

His men laughed, passing comments to each other as the short whore warily unbuttoned her skirt and let it fall to the floor exposing her bare shapely legs. Several of the men whistled and made comments. The small half-moons of her butt shone in the lamplight as she looked at McVain for some relief, but he motioned for her to continue.

"She's got a nice body, huh?" McVain asked Slocum. "Yes."

She slowly raised the blouse above the dark thatch of pubic hair, off the slight swell of her belly pocked by her navel, then cleared the orange-size breasts that shook as she lifted the top off over her head. The men's hurrahing drew an apprehensive look on her olive face as she clutched the blouse to hide her bare torso. Then McVain reached out and snatched it from her grasp. Her mouth formed a small "O" and a wary trapped look filled her brown eyes.

He swung the garment round and round on the end of his finger. Lips pursed, he stared hard at Slocum—waiting for an answer.

"Take her, Slocum," he finally said. "I'm a generous man. I can buy all that you ever want."

Slocum glanced mildly over at the man and slowly shook

his head. "I can afford my own, thanks."

"What's your price? Every man has one. I could use a man like you in me outfit."

"I get to needing work, I might be around," he said, and started to leave.

"Hell, if he don't want her," the man who had previously held her on his lap said aloud. On his feet, he began to shove down his pants. "By God, I'll take her."

He was cheered on by his cohorts, who then grabbed the girl and in a moment had hoisted her, kicking and loudly protesting, atop a table onto her back. Her invader-to-be hobbled over to his goal with his britches halfway to his knees held up in one hand and his stiff mast clutched in the other.

"Stick it to her, Henry!" one shouted, and the others crowded around to watch the excitement and urge him on.

Slocum headed for the door. Dogs had more manners than this lot of horny cutthroats. The hair on his neck itched as he walked out the batwing doors into the sunlight. McVain was not a man accustomed to being denied. The only positive thought that Slocum held was that the Scot wasn't through trying to bribe him. He pushed out the batwing doors, feeling certain the leader wouldn't shoot him down for refusing his generosity because he still wanted him to join his scalpers.

"Halt, you sumbitch!" The staggering drunk rose from a chair on the porch and blocked Slocum's path, unsteady on his boot heels but still determined to stop him.

When they were face to face, Slocum jerked the pistol from the drunk's grip, drove his knee into the man's crotch, and when he bent over in pain, smashed him over the head with the gun barrel. The drunk fell facedown in a pile. Slocum threw the gun aside. It clattered on the cobblestones as he continued on his way across the square.

"Think on me offer!" McVain shouted from the cantina arch.

Slocum never bothered to answer the Scot.

• • •

He stepped inside her home and closed the door. She came from the back and smiled at him despite the haggard look on her face.

"You look like you just met McVain," she said.

"I could have missed meeting him a helluva lot better."

"You know him?"

"Only by his deeds. He is a vicious man. There were lots of stories about his ways in Kansas and Texas during the last buffalo hunts. He probably stole more hides than he ever killed."

"Was he arrested?"

Slocum laughed softly. "Honey, out there, there was no law but your guns and the men to back you. You protected your own and dealt out justice with a pistol or a Sharps."

"They come here often to cash in their scalps. The captain must be coming soon to buy them."

"Are you safe here with them here?" he asked, holding out his arms.

She dismissed his concern with a wave of her hand and stepped in to his hold. "They don't bother me. I drove a knife in one's belly who thought he wanted me one night. They don't bother me because I dress wounds and dig out arrowheads."

"Those men are hardly more than wolves. Don't take any chances."

"Do you know where McVain got most of his men?"

"No," Slocum said, hugging her, savoring her closeness and rocking on his boot heels.

"They were gringos from the Mexican jails. The captain gets them for him. He finds gringos in jail for murder and rape and tells them they will be shot or they can ride with McVain."

"I'd prefer the shooting."

She nuzzled her face on his chest. "I'm glad you didn't make such a decision."

"I may have already. Just a few minutes ago, I turned down joining his dogs."

Estrallia turned her face up and her tired brown eyes

looked perplexed by his disclosure. "He is a mean man. Watch your back."

"I will," he promised her. "I damn sure will watch my back trail." It wasn't bad enough to have the Chiricahuas out; now he also had McVain to contend with. "Get some rest," he finally said, realizing how tired she was from the night's work. "Was it a boy or girl?"

"A boy. They are doing fine now." She smiled at him with pride.

"I'm going to do some checking today. If those Apaches trade at one of these other villages, maybe I can learn where they are holding this Lucia."

She took his hands in her long slender fingers. They were not the soft hands of some rich dowager, but the working hands of a woman who had struggled to bring life from the womb the night before.

"In Paso, you may learn something. There is a man there by the name of Goldfarb who has a large store." She narrowed her eyes "Be careful, and I promise to be rested and ready for you when you return."

With his fist he gave a soft push to her slender nose, and smiled privately at her. "I'll be back in a day."

She pulled his face to hers and gave him a hard kiss with plenty of promise. When they tore themselves apart, she shoved him toward the door. "Go, I will be waiting for you."

He pulled down his hat by the brim, gave her a hard, searching look to see if she meant it, and then drew in his breath. He could put the ride to Paso off for a day. No, she wanted to be clean and rested for him.

He turned on his heel before any more wild notions took over, grabbed up his saddlebags, rifle, and bedroll, and headed for the stables. He found his horses in the stalls, and asked a small boy for his saddle, bridle, and blankets. The youth rushed off to find them for him. When Slocum looked up, a sleepy, hungover Sergeant Gomez came out of the tack room.

"Oh, señor, I did not know the Señora Tomas was expecting you."

"Why don't you go arrest those gun-shooting scalpers over in the cantina, Gomez?" he asked, smoothing the pads on Buck's back. Then he tossed on the saddle, adjusting it to the animal's withers.

"What gun-shooters?" A blank look spread over Gomez's full face.

"The ones that have been shooting up the town here for the last couple hours." Slocum booted Buck hard with his knee and then drew up the cinch.

"I heard no shots, señor."

"Damn funny thing every cur dog in the place is hiding under a wagon, and ain't been a decent woman at the well to draw water all morning."

"I will check," Gomez said, yawning open his mouth as he put up his suspenders.

"You ain't afraid McVain will tie a tin can to your tail, are you?"

Gomez stuck out his chest. "No one messes with me."

"No," Slocum said as he swung in the saddle and reined Buck around. "Not unless he's a mean sumbitch anyway." Slocum touched his hat to the man, then rode out of the barn and into the sunlighted square.

4

The village of Paso lay along the banks of the crystal-clear Rio Negro Oro. Slocum short-loped Buck down the valley road that wound through the fields of knee-high corn, beans, and sprawling melon vines. The church bells were ringing, and he wondered if their purpose was to tell time or to call parishioners. Some places, the daytime bell ringing warned of imminent attack by Indians or raiders.

He reined up beside two young men walking toward the small town carrying large hoes on their shoulders, and stopped to ask them about the meaning of the bells ringing.

"Saint's Day," the first boy said, and the other nodded, both obviously looking with admiration at the yellow horse Slocum rode.

"Do the Apaches come here to trade often?"

"Are you a *federale*?" the taller boy asked. Both youths were barely over five feet, and Slocum guessed them in their late teens.

"Do I look like a *federale*?"

"No," the boy said, embarrassed. "Yes, Apaches come often to trade in the square. They have much gold."

"I never knew they had a mine," Slocum said, looking hard at the boys as he checked Buck's pumping head. The horse was pawing and anxious to go.

"Oh, señor, the Apaches are not miners; they steal it

from the shipments. They rob the poor people that dig it from the ground."

"So they pay cash?"

"*Sí,*" the boy said, and his partner agreed with a hard nod.

"Have they been here recently?" he asked, casting a speculative look ahead at the low hovels that surrounded the white-plastered church.

The boy shook his head no. "But they should come soon."

Slocum thanked the pair and rode on toward the village of mud-coated huts. Some were constructed with adobe bricks and windows. Large palm-frond-covered *remadas* stood beside the *jacales* to use for summer sleeping and cooking.

He passed several dark-eyed women who looked up from tortilla-making, corn-grinding, or preparing food. He caught their questioning gazes, and touched his hat brim in politeness. A few were pretty, some were too full-faced, and others, with some of their teeth missing, grinned to show him the spaces. A few young women carried great jars of water on their heads, walking straight and tall, eyes ahead. They seemed unaffected by his passing.

Screaming naked brown children, dust on their bare limbs from the road dirt, ran out to shout hello at him. Boys and girls lined up in innocence, nude except maybe for a shirt or small poncho, their sex obvious only by what could be seen below their garments, rather than by their haircuts or the shape of their faces. Accompanied by yellow cur dogs with stiff hair who growled at Buck, but only if there was a way to escape, Slocum figured the village welcoming committee had met him.

The sign on the cantina bore the name of the river, and the Black Bear drawing on the wall was faded. He tied his horse beside some hinnies with sack pads and stirrups for saddles. Mexicans called anything a mule that came from a horse and donkey. But Slocum knew hinnies on sight; they were more horselike in their looks, and resulted from a stud horse mating a jenny rather than a jack-and-mare combination, which mules came from. Where he was raised in Alabama, hinnies were scorned for they were harder to break than mules. Mexicans showed no preference, and called all of them mules.

He ducked to enter the batwing doors and once inside, let his eyes adjust to the dim light. Two vaqueros drank at a table with a young *puta*. They raised their black eyes only for a moment to look at him. The one with the mustache quickly clamped a hand on the girl's arm before she could rise. Obviously this gringo intruder looked more flush with money to buy her favor than two *vaqueros* who rode in on mules. She stayed with them anyway, and they went to laughing about something private.

Slocum stood at the bar with his side turned to the door so he could watch the entrance as well as the ones at the table. He ordered a double from the one-eyed bartender, and then removed a quarlie from his vest. He struck a lucifer under the bar rim, and slowly savored the smoke as he drew in the fire and ignited the small cigar.

"You wish for some company?" the bartender said, and motioned with his head toward the table. "Those hombres have no money. Linda would be glad to show you many things, huh?"

Slocum put a silver dollar on the bar and never looked at the man. He acted engrossed in the dust-clad deer antlers on the wall. "Maybe you could earn some money." He removed the quarlie from his mouth. "Tell me about the Apaches that come to trade in this town. Maybe you can earn that dollar if I hear enough that I want to hear about them."

"You can see the army does not guard this village. The government says we must pay for them if they send some soldiers here. These people are poor farmers, what can we pay?" He dropped his head and put the glass he'd polished under the counter, then rose up with another to shine.

"Señor Goldfarb said, the hell with the army. We would make our own treaty with the Apaches." He shrugged. "So they come and trade here. They never rape our women or raid our crops. They bring gold to buy things."

"Blood money?" Slocum asked between drags.

"Maybe, maybe not. There are not deaths in this village. We do not hide under our beds at night, fearful that some Apache will sneak in our houses and cut our privates off and stuff them in our mouth before we die and then they rape our wives and daughters, huh?"

"This Goldfarb, he makes much money off this treaty?"

"So do the farmers. They can sell their beans and corn at good price. They often trade horses and mules to the Apache. The Apache will buy woven wool. What does the army buy from us?"

"Nothing, I guess. Where is this Goldfarb?"

"At his store. Maybe he takes a siesta at this time."

"When is the next trade day?" Slocum rested his fingertips on the silver dollar. He acted undecided about which way he would push it.

The bartender looked in his direction with the blind eye, the one with the scarred pupil, and shook his head that he could not or would not say. Slowly Slocum drew the silver dollar back towards himself.

The bartender leaned closer and, after noting who was in the place, whispered, "Tomorrow."

"How do I know you aren't lying?"

"The bells—they ring to tell them there is no army close by," he said, close enough that Slocum could smell his bad breath.

Good enough. Slocum shoved the silver dollar across to the man. "Have you seen the Don's daughter riding with the bucks. Lucia Salisar?"

"*Sí*. She rode with them last time." The man resumed his polishing.

"Was she tied up."

"No."

Slocum scrubbed the perspiration off his mouth with his palm. Strange thing. She was a prisoner and not bound. Maybe they had her so scared that she didn't dare make a move.

"Did she look sad?"

The bartender shrugged. "I couldn't say. I only saw her among a bunch of riders."

"Thanks." Slocum downed the liquor that burned like fresh lava scorching his throat. He set the glass on the bar with a deep exhale, touched his hat for the benefit of the blue-eyed girl seated between the two *vaqueros,* then headed for the door.

Goldfarb's store was an impressive two-story structure. No windows on the first floor, and cell-like iron gates were open outside the handsome green wooden ones that were swung inward. Slocum paused to shove his hat up with his thumb and examine the doors' artwork. The thick wood was alive with carvings of some kind of monkeys with horns and voluptuous maidens with little clothing. Obviously these strange baboons were some kind of guards for the women, for they perched above the maidens, who danced about in garden like settings.

"Gargoyles! They are keepers of the gate," a man with a deep voice said.

He wore a great white silk robe that concealed perhaps three hundred or more pounds. Bald, his head shone like it had been polished, and his eyes were deep-set and almost pink. His white lashes were almost invisible on his pale skin.

"And what can I get for you, sir," he said in impeccable English that Slocum tried to place from a particular region. Maybe Boston, maybe Philadelphia—the man's diction was too correct.

"Where do these critters live at?" Slocum asked, his curiosity stirred by the carvings.

"In one's imagination, I suppose. They are animals of myth, sir. Like the Sphinx on the Nile. There never was a half-man-half-lion, though the pharaohs of Egypt tried repeatedly in experiments to produce one through the mating of man and lioness."

"Hope they declawed her first," Slocum said with a smile.

"Yes, that would be necessary for me to mount one. How about a real cigar?"

"Fine, but my business transactions here may be so small that you find your offer is too generous."

"Let me be the judge. Come, let us sit in chairs. I find so few civilized men in this corner of the world that I am honored for a few moments of conversation when one comes by." He pointed to a glass jar of cigars, and a shapely girl of perhaps twenty years old appeared and with a bow presented the long black cigar.

As she bent over to offer the cigar, her low-cut blouse fell open enough to expose her hard teardrop breasts. Slocum took the cigar with a quiet thank-you. She straightened with a small private smile in the corner of her mouth at what she read in Slocum's eyes. She walked back to the counter with a hypnotizing swing of her hips, making it hard for him to think about lighting his cigar. Finally he cut the end off with his jackknife.

"My wife Ruby," Goldfarb said.

"A lovely lady, you are very lucky," Slocum said as he reached down and struck a match on the pegged floor.

"Yes, but we did not come to speak of wives. I detect a Southern dialect in your words?"

"Alabama."

"You have lost much of that, though, haven't you?"

Slocum agreed, and drew deep on the rich cigar. It was a fine expensive tobacco product with medicinal powers to calm him as he lounged back in the chair.

"What brings you to Paso?"

"A man wants his daughter back from the Apaches." Cigar in hand, Slocum stared hard at the big man across from him.

"That stupid Don Sallisar?"

"Yes, he hired me to bring her back. Seems his wife is distraught about the girl. Says he paid the reward they asked for her and they didn't deliver her."

"Maybe they want another reward."

"I warned him of that."

"He is a big landowner. He pays many *pistoleros*. Why

doesn't he lead his own men into the mountains and take her away from her captors?''

Slocum nipped on the cigar. The sharp sweetness tasted good on his tongue. ''Perhaps he feared they might kill the girl.''

''No, sir, I suspect he is a coward. On the one hand, he wants the daughter returned, but at no risk to himself. So he hires a soldier of fortune who comes riding by. Is that the story so far?''

''I never saw the man before, but a friend asked me to help him.''

''My name is Lester, Lester Goldfarb. If you would rather not give me yours it is of no concern, and I must apologize I was so excited to discover you admiring the door that I forgot my manners.''

''No problem. Mine's Slocum.''

''Slocum, nice to meet a civilized person in a land of dolts and ignorance.''

''Whose band is she with?''

Goldfarb shrugged, and the great silk robe made a wave like lake water propeled by a sudden wind. ''How am I to know?''

''Let's get to the point. Apaches come here to trade and you have seen this girl with them.''

''Is he paying you that much?''

''Enough.''

''There are many leaders today.''

''I know, I spoke to Natise a few days back.''

''Ah, yes, but there are more—Geronimo, Chato, and even Tomatoes.''

''Tomatoes?'' Slocum frowned at the man. Strange name for an Apache. He was unfamiliar with that one.

''Ah, he is addicted to the canned ones. But make no mistake, he is as tough as the others.''

Slocum settled back in his chair recalling the Apaches surrender on the border almost five years before. Geronimo was the hard-eyed one with the sharp nose. Chato smiled a lot and liked to joke, but he was also the one who could turn as cold as stone. Natise was handsome but much smaller than his father. And this Tomatoes was a new one who had come up the ranks since then. *They had many leaders. . . .*

"Don't be so quick to judge us," Goldfarb said, breaking into Slocum's thoughts about the past.

"I'm not judging anyone. I've got a job to do."

"Oh, I can see behind those green eyes. You are saying this fat rich merchant is selling them arms and food so they can kill others."

"I understand there is a truce with the Apaches that these people figure is worth more than any peso you make off the deal."

Goldfarb nodded. "Let us have some civilized whiskey." He made a sign to his wife, and she brought a bottle of bonded rye and two glasses. She set them on the table and then excused herself.

"Open it, Slocum. I save such luxury for special occasions."

Slocum looked at the label: Tennessee whiskey, made from cool limestone cave water and the dark nutlike rye grain fermented in great vats, distilled over hardwood fires and aged in charred oak barrels. The thought of such fine liquor filled his mouth with saliva.

"I can see that you agree with my choice of women and whiskey anyhow." Goldfarb laughed at Slocum's expense.

"Which band is she with?"

"The pretty daughter of the Don?" he asked, accepting the glass of whiskey from Slocum.

"That's who I'm here for." Slocum sipped the liquor and looked hard across the rim of the glass at the man for an answer.

"Tomatoes's bunch, I think."

Slocum crossed his legs and sat back, savoring the richness of the rye. "Is he coming here tomorrow?"

"Probably, but—" Goldfarb held up a single finger— "one thing, you cannot do is take her back while they are here, or we will stop you. Whatever it takes. Including killing you if necessary. This is part of our treaty with them."

"Go on," Slocum said, knowing the man had more to say.

"If we break the treaty or let anyone else break it, then all our lives are in danger for they will turn on us like mad dogs. The women and children first, because they would be easy to kill."

"I understand," Slocum said. This twist would definitively change his plans. He had simply intended to take her from them while all the trading was going on and her captors were distracted.

He needed a new strategy. Maybe by morning and the arrival of the Apaches, he would think up a better plan to take her away from them. If not, there would be a way to do it later. He settled in the chair to enjoy the man's whiskey and conversation.

He watched the deep frown on Goldfarb's face that mention of the name "McVain" brought, and noted the man's disapproval of the scalpers in general. When Slocum informed the storekeeper that they were probably in Santa Cristo to collect for their latest batch of hair, the man was visibly upset.

"We shall watch the road better," Goldfarb said, deep in his own thoughts.

There must have been bad blood between Goldfarb and McVain. But Slocum did not pursue it. He had enough problems of his own. Like Lucia Sallisar, the captive—or was she?

5

The apartment that Goldfarb had provided for Slocum's overnight stay was to the west side of the second floor, so as Slocum listened to the roosters herald the dawn, he could not see the main street. In the long shadows that spilled on the ground below, he could see an assortment of hipshot horses in the alley beneath his sill. From the array of saddles and tack he guessed some of the Apaches were already there to trade.

He watched an Indian return with several chickens; then the buck tried to tie them to his saddlehorn in a cloud of feathers and squawking. The man finally succeeded. He stomped around brushing the coating of feathers off his blue army shirt, making a snowstorm. Finished, he went off bowlegged for the front of the store again.

Slocum eased himself down the hallway to the head of the stairs, where he could sit and observe the store full of Apaches. With unblocked hats and kerchief head coverings, some even wearing feathers in headbands, they moved among the trade goods. Most of their women were hatless.

"I don't know if they'll fit or not," a man in the crowd said, holding up a pair of shoes.

"Try them on!" Goldfarb shouted.

Slocum spotted her. She wore a muted Navajo blanket over her head, and had she not turned so he could see the beauty in her face, he might have missed her. Lucia Sallisar stood along the wall in the background. There was no doubt who she was, even with the blanket for a mantle, in the crowd of men and women going over the store goods. He wished he could see more of her. Was she pregnant? Her father had said he didn't care about her condition.

No one acted like her guard. It was as he had planned: the perfect place for him to take her. As he sat on top of the stairs, it was hard for him not to do something about rescuing her while the Apaches were so distracted in their trading. He almost laughed as a large squaw tried to put a cast-iron skillet under her dress and conceal it.

Soon many of the Apaches began laughing at the woman, until she brandished the article in both hands and threatened to permanently end their laughter. Goldfarb waded over with a smaller skillet and presented it to her, as if to soothe her anger. She left, skillet in hand, without a word, but many stinging-sounding Apache words from others in the store followed her retreat.

Goldfarb was no fool, and the shoplifting would no doubt raise the prices the others would pay. Presenting the iron pot was a way to smooth out any problems. Like children, the Indians lived by different rules than white men. Slocum knew that from the days he had spent in Cochise's camp.

When he looked again, the girl was gone. Damn, he had been distracted and missed who took her outside. He did not know any of the Indians, nor could he distinguish a leader in the store. Apaches were very independent. They did not take orders, they followed some one they liked or respected, But even a chief could not say for one man to go kill another man. Direct orders were not given unless they met in council and someone volunteered.

Goldfarb and his employees worked hard to tend to the customers; much gold dust tipped their brass scales. Some money flowed from red to white hands, but the main currency was the precious metal. The Apaches seemed to have good supply of it that came in various pouches. No doubt dead men's earnings.

An older man came to the bottom of the stairs. He wore

a headband, and his shoulder-length hair was streaked in gray. At the stairs, he stopped and looked up.

"I have seen you before," he said in good English, squinting to look up the dimly lighted stairs with the glare of the room lamps in his eyes.

"Cochise's camp," Slocum said, not offering to rise or greet the man.

The man nodded. Satisfied that his question had been answered, he turned on his rawhide heel and went back to shop. He stopped before another tribesman and jerked a thumb up to indicate Slocum's position. The buck nodded to his words, but never looked Slocum's way. Slocum's concern passed without an incident.

This was the band of Apaches that held the Sallisar girl. He had learned that much. Where their *rancheria* was located was the next question.

"Señor, I have some breakfast," Ruby said with a large wooden tray in her arms.

"Sorry," Slocum said, rising to his feet. "I found the trading interesting to observe from up here."

She nodded that she understood. "Come with me," she said.

"Whose band is down there now?"

"I think they are with the one called Tomatoes."

"I don't know him. Who is he?"

She shrugged her shoulders as she opened double glass French doors to a balcony and set the tray on a table. "Here, have a place to sit, señor."

"Tomatoes is a young one," she said, straightening her blouse as she stood before him. "They say he is meaner than the others. He is tall as you are, but broader." She indicated Slocum's shoulders.

"Will you join me?" Slocum asked, indicating the spread of eggs, *corizzo,* and tortillas.

"No, I must get back to work. There is never enough help on such days."

"Describe this Tomatoes to me, so if I see him I will know him."

"He is very nice-looking. Some say his mother was

Mexican. He is very strong and has a scar on his cheek."
She pointed to the left side of her face and traced where it
would be on him. "They say some cruel white men did
that to him when he was little."

"Thanks, Ruby," Slocum said as he looked beyond the
garden below to the blue, hazy Madres. Nothing for a dollar
was ever easy, he realized as he considered the browned
pork, frijoles, fresh-chopped tomatoes and greenery as well
as the stack of corn tortillas. The steaming mug of coffee
held his attention long enough to sip it. Then he set it down
and began to eat. Getting Lucia Sallisar back was not to be
an easy task.

After his breakfast, Slocum remained inconspicuous. Seated
on a bench in the shade out front, he observed the various
bands coming and going. Natise and his people came,
traded, and left. Natise ignored him.

In late afternoon, Slocum had taken a place on the bench
before the store. He watched a small man ride up the plaza
at the head of a group of men and women. At the hitch
rack, the man drew rein and with eagle eyes searched about
the village. He carried a Winchester decorated with brass
tacks and wore a small skullcap. Like a cat, he dismounted
lithely. On the steps, he paused and looked hard at Slocum,
who had both elbows on his knees, using his Barlow to
shave cedar slivers from a branch.

"You bring the gawdamn Army with you?" he demanded, stopping short in his tracks.

Slocum shook his head. "No, Geronimo, I do not work
for them now."

"You were with Nantan Lupan at the place of the
Skull."

"He is not my chief now."

"You're gawdamn lucky."

"Is that so?"

"I will kill that bearded bastard and anyone rides for
him if he comes to these mountains!" The Apache shook
the rifle muzzle in Slocum's face. "He is not a ghost. You

tell him to stay up there.'' He pointed north toward Arizona.

"I can't tell him nothing.''

"You tell him that I will cut out his eyes if he comes to Mexico.''

"Tell him yourself. He will come.''

"He lied to us.''

"I don't think he lied. I think others may have, but Crook did not lie to you.''

"Only a dog or a Papago would live at San Carlos. Give that place to our enemies.''

Slocum simply nodded. There was not a damn thing he could do, but if this short chieftain wanted to express his anger over the U.S. Indian policy, let him. Slocum would simply whittle on the cedar until the anger passed.

"You hear me, white eyes?''

"I heard the great chief of the Chiricahua.''

"What is your business here?''

Slocum wanted to say, "None of your damn business,'' but instead said, "I am looking for gold.''

"I have gold,'' the Apache said, drawing a long buckskin pouch from his breechcloth. "Take mine.''

Slocum simply shook his head. "I will find my own.''

"I think you lie about looking for gold, I think you are here to tell Nantan Lupan where we are.''

Slocum denied it with a head shake. "He don't need me to tell him a damn thing. He knows that you headed here in the first place.''

Geronimo grinned. Then he shouted for the others to dismount, go inside, and shop, that this white eyes was no threat to Chiricahuas. And with that he marched inside at the head of his entourage.

Arms loaded with items from blankets to food, they repeatedly came in and out to fill panniers and sacks tied to saddlehorns. With hardly a sideways look at Slocum, squaws and bucks worked hard to complete their trade day. Finally Geronimo came out and stood on the stairs.

"Slo-cum?'' the Apache asked.

Slocum pushed his Stetson up with a thumb and acknowledged the chief.

"You tell Nantan Lupan you saw my band. They all have good guns and many shells. They will die in these mountains rather than go back to San Carlos and live with those dogs."

Slocum took the stick he had been working on and pointed it north. "No need in me telling him anything. I figure he's coming this way soon enough. You can tell him yourself."

Geronimo spat in the dirt close to Slocum's boot. "That is what I say to him."

He and his band mounted up and rode toward the mountains. Slocum sat for a long while shaving cedar. Goldfarb came out and stood in the doorway, the hot afternoon breeze wafting the ankle-long silk robe around his great form.

"They don't look half as deadly as they are, do they?" Goldfarb said.

"Nope," Slocum said, hearing the voices of the village children again for the first time that day. They were back in the street, rolling hoops, and some were dragging a sleepy burro out of the alley. Their shouts and yells signaled that all was normal again.

Slocum rose and stretched.

"Come inside. Time for more rye," his host said.

Slocum folded his Barlow shut and nodded. He had still not seen this chief Tomatoes, nor did he know the location of their *rancheria*. What about the girl? Was she already someone's wife?

He glanced around the street. Paso had returned to normal. Women were getting water at the well, and their naked brown children rushed about in shrill voices.

He frowned as the two *vaqueros* appeared in a hurry when they left the cantina. They mounted their mules, whipped them into a trot, and rode west as if toward Santa Cristo. Maybe their time off was over and they had to get back to some hacienda. Strange that they'd stayed so long into the day and then left so late in the afternoon. He shrugged off the notion and followed his host inside. His mouth watered at the prospect of the good whiskey.

"Oh, señor, it is dangerous in those canyons," the youth begged with wide brown eyes.

Slocum had located the young Juan Herrera, whom Goldfarb had spoken of as a possible guide. Herrera had been kidnapped as a boy and held for several years by the Apaches. His knowledge of that part of the mountains could make him invaluable as a scout. Slocum squatted on his boot heels in the hot dirt. The knee-high corn around them rustled in the dry wind as the boy leaned on his hoe handle.

"I can pay you five pesos for guiding me up there, Juan," Slocum said.

"Have you ever seen what they do to their enemies?" The boy's look of fear grew larger as he waited for Slocum's answer.

"I know all about them. Once we locate Tomatoes' camp, you can come right back here."

"If I am alive. Señor, I lived for six years with them. I know their fierceness."

"Ten pesos then."

"But I can only lead you close to them and then I must leave you." His dark brown eyes questioned Slocum.

"Good enough, we start out at dawn," Slocum said. "I will have a horse for you to ride."

The boy made the sign of a cross, then looked skyward with his hands pressed together. "Mother of God be with us. I will meet you then. But if they kill you—"

"I'll take my chances."

He pushed himself to his feet and headed for Buck, who stood ground-tied at the end of the corn row. Slocum hated the time he'd lost locating this youth. It simply took a lot of time to get things going. Maybe in a few days he could locate the Apaches' camp and figure out how to extract Lucia from them. There was plenty for him to do to get ready to leave.

•   •   •

The evening breezes came down the canyon and cooled Paso at night. Slocum sat with his host Goldfarb on the balcony, and they drank his good whiskey.

"Do you recall the two men who were in the cantina a couple days ago?" Goldfarb asked, leaning over to fill his glass.

"Two *vaqueros,* one thin-faced, the other looked younger, why?"

"The bartender came to me this evening. He thinks they were spies for McVain and his scalpers."

"I had wondered why they rode out after Geronimo left. Do they know about the bell business?"

The big man pursed his lips together and shrugged his thick shoulders under the robe. "Anyone can add one and one, come out with two, even scalpers. I have sent for the *puta* Linda to see what she heard."

"Does she know anything?"

"Probably."

They drank in silence until the girl arrived; then both men stood up and Goldfarb indicated a seat for her opposite them.

"This is Señor Slocum," he said, indicating him as they resumed their seats.

"Nice to meet you, señor." She looked even younger than she had in the bar. "You were in the cantina two days ago."

"You were busy." He smiled at her.

"Not tonight," she said wishfully. "Oh, I am sorry, Señor Goldfarb. Rudy said that you wished to know about the men that came here. One's name was Vargas, and he bragged he was from El Paso and owned a big casa there."

"Did he mention what he did for a living?" Goldfarb asked.

She crossed her legs and let a good portion of her shapely calf show. "Oh, he said he hated dirty damn Indians. Once he hushed that boy up when he was drunk and telling how they used Indian women like they were such great lovers."

"You didn't hear how they did it?" Goldfarb asked, acting amused at her words.

"Oh, it was all lies anyway. They were not such men. They could never do such things to any woman. They were made like little boys." She held up her little finger to demonstrate their size, and then shook her head in disgust.

The three laughed as she turned her palms up and shook her head in a helpless expression. It was obvious from her opinion that these men were not very adequate to the task.

"Did they ever mention a man called McVain?" Goldfarb asked.

She stared out into space, then finally shook her head.

"Thank you, Linda," Goldfarb said, and tossed her a coin as she rose to excuse herself.

She wrinkled her small nose as she caught it in midair. "I could earn this." Then she looked at Slocum.

"My guest has to leave very early," Goldfarb declared. "Good evening."

Slocum told her the same as he rose and said maybe another time. She gave a shrug and left them. He watched her disappear down the dimly lighted hall.

"What will you do now?" Goldfarb asked, settling down and pouring them another glass of rye.

"I will go look for the girl. You have a month to make plans."

"Just know that McVain will do anything especially for the scalps of those chiefs like Natise and Geronimo. And any others with black hair, Apache or not."

Slocum agreed. He sat back and considered going after the girl. At dawn, he must head for the mountains. That wouldn't be long. He raised the glass to Goldfarb's health and then drank deep.

6

The canyon walls rose above them like great organ pipes scoured by wind and water that towered to dazzling heights. In the cool shadows of early morn the pair rode up the narrow dry-wash floor; the click of their horses echoed sharply, as did the cry of the harpy eagle, soaring high overhead. Only small bushes clung tenaciously to the sparse soil, lest the next flood wipe them out of existence when turbulent water cleansed the narrow throat of the deep chasm.

"Did you learn much when you lived with the Apaches?" Slocum asked the boy who rode ahead on the livery horse.

"I was too busy wanting to go home. I think you know how young boys are."

"How did you get free?" Slocum asked, studying the boy's back and curious about his obvious distaste for the Apache life.

"My uncle paid them four horses for me."

"Your parents?"

"Dead. They and my grandparents were killed in the raid, when they kidnapped me. For many years, I thought no one knew I was in the Apache camp. Then one day I was free."

"You must like your uncle."

"Oh, yes. I will buy two horses with your money and pay him back."

"What did you do in the Apache camp."

"I learned to eat rats." Juan shook his shoulders in revulsion.

Slocum laughed aloud at his reaction. "I guess rats, squirrels, rabbits are all the same when you skin them."

"Not to a boy," Juan said with a shake of his head.

"I lived on rattlesnakes one time for a week."

"What did they taste like?"

"Chicken."

"That's what rat tasted like."

The temperature began to rise, and the canyon became an oven as the day pressed on. A whiff of pine-scented air on the wind swirled down the confines for their first breath of relief. Slocum felt confident they would soon reach the top, though he took no chance by repeatedly searching the cliffs and what he could see ahead and behind for anyone or anything out of place.

Finally they emerged from the confines of the canyon onto a windswept knob. Slocum stood up in the stirrups to let the cool breeze sweep his sweaty face and draw out the heat. They let their horses blow and studied the thin hogback that let across the open sky to the distant range. The narrow bridgelike structure looked like a place for goats to cross, in Slocum's opinion. Either side of the single footpath was straight down in a sheer thousand feet of rocky precipice. He forced a deep swallow and remounted Buck to cross the mile or so of thin air that led to the face of the mountain.

"No place to slip," he reminded his horse, and stared ahead as they set out.

"We're lucky," Juan said.

"How is that?" he asked, twisting slightly in the saddle to check their backtrail. Nothing back there. He settled down in the seat, still waiting for an answer from the boy.

"The wind is usually so bad up here you have to lead your horse afoot across this thing for fear of getting blown off."

"No, thanks, I believe I'd stay home that day," Slocum said, and wished they were already on the other side.

"There's a stream in that side canyon over there." Juan pointed in the direction where the mountain creased as they continued single-file across the ridge back.

"Good, we can let the horses get a bellyful of grass and a drink there. They'll need it."

Ahead the boy's horse stumbled on his front foot and went to his knees. Slocum checked Buck, watching Juan carefully. The wind had grow stronger and whistled in Slocum's ear as he waited for the boy's reaction. Buck shifted under him, causing some gravel to take off for the long fall.

Juan gingerly lifted his horse's head, and his mount recovered to his feet. Slocum drew in a deep breath and then slowly exhaled again. Buck shuffled with a little impatience that caused Slocum to check him. He patted the big horse on the neck to reassure him. Then they continued their crossing.

It was like being an eagle up there, Slocum decided, except they didn't have wings. Finally they drew near the mountain connection, and he could see a shelf of ground where he intended to dismount and stomp his boots on solid rock. Buck finally scrambled up the loose talus rocks and they were there. Slocum slid out of the saddle and let his legs gain some strength before he released the saddlehorn.

The horses shook as if they too were grateful to be across the narrow pathway. Slocum looked back at the trail, pitched like a steep roof peak disappearing into thin obscurity. He was grateful for the boy's guidance. He might have never ventured across such a dangerous path, thinking he had lost the savages' trail. He remounted and followed Juan, anxious for the drink of water.

They rode under some jack pines, and he could see the sparkle of the stream deep in the canyon. Like a diamond band it rushed over house-size rocks and deadfalls from past floods. Soon the sound of the water told of the force that bore it from the mountains.

"This creek will have trout in it!" Slocum shouted at his discovery.

"The Apaches say the fish in these waters will make you sick."

"Listen, boy, Apaches don't know a damn thing about trout. I'll show you something better than rats to eat." Slocum booted Buck toward the walnut tree growing in the flat portion of the creek bottom.

"Whoa, Buck," he coaxed as he rose up and finally stood atop his saddle to picked an armful of green walnuts. Then he dumped them on the ground and took a sack from his saddlebags.

"Get your shoes off and get in that rapids over there below the pool. There will be fish coming out for you to catch." He dismounted and undid the cinch to turn Buck loose to graze.

"Catch? But we have no net or hooks." The youth looked in complete dismay.

"Just do as I say," Slocum said as he sat down on the ground to pull off his boots.

Soon he had the walnuts and some rocks for ballast in the sack with his lariat tied to the end. He grinned at the boy, who was half-shin-deep in the riffle below the pool. With a wild swing Slocum sent the sack out into the pool. With a great splash, it settled under the surface.

"Watch for them!" he shouted to Juan.

The boy shrugged, looking as if he felt very stupid with his white pants rolled up standing in the stream waiting. Then he shouted, "A fish is coming."

"Get him," Slocum yelled, and reeled in the sack. "There will be more," he said, and gimped over the sharp rocks to join Juan in the run.

A dull-acting silver trout came out of the pool barely able to swim, and Slocum grasped his muscular form in his hand. With a toss it was soon flopping on the bank with Juan's fish. Finally, with six nice fat trout on the bank, the men waded out of the water.

"Will the others recover?" Juan asked about sluggish fish that they had missed coming out of the pool.

"In this freshwater supply, yes," Slocum said as he reeled out his sack and recoiled his rope. He joined the boy and knelt by the stream to help him clean their catch.

"Where did you learn this?" Juan asked.

"My uncle showed me this years ago when I was younger than you. Something in the green walnuts does it."

Juan, with a gutted fish in his hand, studied the stately walnut tree. He shook his head when he turned back to look at Slocum. "Beats all how quick it worked."

"It worked," Slocum said, busy slitting open another fish's belly. He had spent all his youth fishing or hunting to avoid school studies or farmwork.

They cooked the fish over a small fire on green willow spits. When they finished their meal, both of them were full of trout and cool water as they gathered their horses to ride on.

They climbed another range into the Madres by the time the sun chose to drown itself far west in the Sea of Cortez. Hard jerky, with canteen water to wash it down, was their supper. They left their horses saddled, tied on ropes so they could move out in a hurry. Each wrapped in a blanket against the mountain night cold, Slocum and Juan slept until the morning doves heralded dawn and they got up with burning eyes to capture their horses and cinch up.

They rode southward until midday, when Juan dismounted and checked some signs on the broad crest of a range. He followed it on foot for a ways leading his horse, and then he drew up in a grove of jack pines.

"This is where I leave you," he said.

"I don't see any camp." Slocum made a thorough search of the mountain top—there was nothing.

"They're in that canyon." Juan pointed to the side. "You will find them there."

"If I don't find the camp," Slocum said sternly as he rose in the stirrups, "you owe me twice this money I am paying you."

They must be close, for the boy was acting very upset waiting for his money. Slocum's threat had fallen on deaf ears. Still, nothing he could see indicated the Apaches were anywhere nearby. Maybe the boy knew, or maybe his fear of them finally had ate him up. He certainly hadn't liked living with them as a young boy, that was for sure.

Slocum drew the money from his pants pocket with a grave look. "You better be right."

"I am," the boy said, taking the money and thanking him. He quickly remounted, rode off to the north at a trot, and did not look back.

Slocum took Buck to a glade on the far side of the mountain. He tied him on the long rope to graze.

"Don't make a fuss over here, horse, or you may end up as the main dish them Apaches have tonight. They really like to eat fat horses," he told Buck aloud with a serious head shake, hoping his words never came true.

Next he hid his saddle in a deadfall, then took the brass scope, saddlebags, and rifle. Still not convinced the boy had told him the truth, he skirted to the north side of the side canyon that Juan had pointed out, and was working his way downhill through the tall pine timber when he spotted a red flash far below in the spot where the boy had said the Apache would be.

He dropped to his belly and peered through the scope among the pine needles. He discovered a red-mantled squaw and the corner of a wickiup in his eyepiece. His heart quickened. He had to go all the way down there undetected and locate the girl, because there was no way to see her from up here.

He stashed his saddlebags and rifle in a downed top. Tree by tree, he began his descent, hoping none of the Apaches spotted him. His breath short, he placed his feet carefully each time he stepped on the steep side of the mountain. One dislodged rock and he would be Apache bait, spread over a red anthill or hung over a fire until his brains boiled. He had seen both examples of Apache torture. No, they would never let him live.

The next tree trunk and he would be on a flat bench in the mountain. Halfway to his next appointed spot of concealment, he heard the nearby laughter of a woman! He was caught in the open, and there was nothing to do but hit the pine needles and figure a way to crawl out of sight before he was discovered.

His heart pounding in his throat, Slocum watched a young buck and girl swing around a tree base not fifty feet away. She was trying to escape his nuzzling on her neck as he forced her against the tree. Her hand reached down for his manhood. At her discovery, she gave a small cry. He let out a coyote yell at her grasp, which Slocum figured would bring the entire camp up on the mountain. But her palm cupped over his mouth quickly silenced him. Then he raised her blouse and began to suckle on her globelike breast.

She finally pried him loose and drew him up as her hands stripped away his loincloth and his copper butt soon shone in the shafts of sunlight coming through the dense canopy. With his manhood in her fist, he eagerly worked up her skirt. Then she raised a shapely leg for his entrance. A sharp cry escaped her mouth as he entered her, his strong hands grasped the half-moon cheeks of her butt holding her in position as he plunged into her with the power of a locomotive. Both of them sought pleasure in wild abandonment. Out of breath, they gasped for air without stopping. The maiden's back hard against the tree, she clung to his shoulders as the passion grew wilder and heaved her hips toward him. In a newfound fury, he plunged in and out of her in complete abandonment.

The buck's final cry of ecstasy came as Slocum made good his snakelike escape behind a huge log. He lay with his nose buried in the sour dead pine needles as the maiden gave a scream of satisfaction, then a sharp inhale as she swallowed her breath and passion's daze swarmed over both of them.

Shit! This was all he needed, Slocum decided as he lay as close as he could get to the huge rotten log.

Darkness engulfed the canyon, only the light of the small fires illuminated giant shadows on the hillsides when someone passed by one. Less than a hundred yards from the nearest wickiup, Slocum could hear the trickle of a creek that ran between him and the camp. His mouth dry as cotton, Slocum waited on his belly as the men sang war songs and a drummer beat out his rhythm.

Thump. Thump. The sound carried up the dark canyon choked with tall pine timber as the drummer beat the taunt dry hide. Some shaman cried for divine intervention, and turtle-shell rattles answered him. Nearby several men chanted, and they sounded like a pack of sick coyotes to Slocum.

He needed a drink of water as bad as anything. Perhaps the Apaches had lost all their dogs in the move to the Madres. They were not ones to become attached to any animals, and dogs sometimes were prone to bark when Army troops rode by the Apaches' position. He hoped there were no dogs in the camp.

He had counted about a dozen grass wickiups, but the one where they held the girl was not obvious. Earlier a few children had splashed in the creek, but now only the adults were awake, singing and chanting.

Soon he heard bells and shuffle of soles on the gritty ground. They must be dancing, he decided, unable to see them for the wickiups were in the way and the poor light didn't help. The Apaches never built big fires for fear of detection.

He drew in a deep breath as he studied some movement coming out of the camp. He finally saw her step from the shadows below him and move into the starlight that slanted through the pines. It was Lucia Sallisar, no doubt by herself. And her purpose was obvious as she removed her mantle. She had come to bath.

Was anyone close to her? He saw nothing except the dancers grew louder. Obvious this was a celebration with *tiswain,* a liquor that Indians made from the century plant roots. They were denied it on the reservation, a particular point of contention.

"Why, we have made it all our lives," Juh had indignantly told Crook at Skull Canyon.

"I don't care how much damn *tiswain* you made in your life," Crook had said, impatient with the chief's insistence, slicing the air with his flat hand and arm. "Apaches can't make any more of it. You get wild and do crazy things when you drink it."

In the Sierra Madres, they had no master to keep them from making their favorite beverage. Like children, sneak a smoke behind a barn, they obviously would flaunt their liberty in the wilds of Mexico.

He watched with interest as Lucia shed her blouse. In the milky light, her pear-shaped breasts glowed. Next, she wiggled off the skirt, then stood in the bluish light long enough for him to draw in a deep settling of breath—he hoped.

She stepped into the water, testing it. It was obviously cold, for she hugged herself, but undaunted by the temperature, she continued into the small pool until the water reached her knees.

Where was her guard? Slocum studied all around as the sounds of the celebration grew noisier and the participants shouted louder by each passing minute.

Somehow he had to capture her and head back for Buck. They must cover over a mile or more up the cow-faced mountainside to the horse. No small task, and all this before she was missed and the Apaches took up pursuit.

If they were drunker, maybe he could escape them. Apaches hated the night, but they weren't fools either. Still, they had some sort of belief that if they were killed in the night then their souls would roam forever in eternity and not reach Apache heaven.

But if he stole their most prized captive, they were bound to follow his backtrail. He was two days hard ride from civilization, and he could only imagine retracing his way across the narrow hogback in the dark. The splash of water made him realize he must do something quickly.

He rose to his hands and feet. When she came out of the water he had to take her, and then convince her that he was friendly as well as ready to save her. A knot formed in the pit of his empty belly. Anything like a scream from her and they would have the whole band down there.

Dripping water, she rose to her feet in the pearl light that shone on her ivory skin. Slocum was already moving like a coyote down the slope and keeping to the shadows. He tried to swallow the hard fist in his throat—he had one chance to pull this off.

7

"No!" she protested as his hand closed over her mouth. She was stronger than he expected. He looked quickly at the camp to see if one of the shouting dancers had come running. But they probably never heard it as the muscular Lucia tried to wrestle free of his grasp.

"Hush, your father sent me to get you out of here," he hissed in her ear.

She went almost limp for a minute; he carefully uncovered her mouth.

"I don't want to leave," she said in a loud whisper.

"You don't—" What the hell should he do? Take her or let her stay with them? He glanced in the direction of the wickiups. The fire had grown brighter, for he could see the orange light reaching higher into the sky and the participants were even louder. Loud enough to give him cold chills up his spine as they screamed bloodcurdling cries into the night.

"Girl, your mother cries every day for you," he said.

She dropped her head in defeat. "For that I am sorry."

"Come, we don't have much time. I have a horse over the hill. Those bucks will soon discover you are gone and they'll be on our trail."

"Who are you anyway?" she asked, looking at him hard.

"That ain't necessary now. Come on." he said, casting

another glance over his shoulder.

"You aren't one of my father's *pistoleros,*" she said in a low voice as she let him pull her after him. "They would never have slipped up on an Apache camp and got me. How long have you been out here?"

"Long enough to see you bathing. But that wasn't my purpose," he said under his breath as they paused to catch their breath on the bench where earlier the pair had made love.

"Well, you certainly aren't a gentleman," she said in a huff.

"Wasn't any time for that, missy." He could still hear the war whoops and the sounds of dancing. "Let's go, we've got miles to cover."

"What if I don't go with you?"

"I'll have to hogtie you and throw you over my shoulder," he said, impatient with her threats.

"I'll scream bloody murder."

"I'll gag you. Come on!" He jerked her by the arm. They didn't have time for all this foolish arguing.

"Who are you?" she asked, coming along but not without some pulling on his part.

"My name's Slocum. I work for your father. Now quit dragging your heels and come along or I will throw you over my shoulder. You leave a husband back there?"

She threw her head back and laughed aloud. Loud enough he wanted to slap his hand over her mouth and cut her off.

"Hush," he said.

"Oh, they are all getting so drunk, they won't hear a thing."

"Yes and bloodthirsty too. You never answered my question," he said, and pulled her after him.

"No, I have no Apache husband."

"Good."

"Why?" she asked.

"Because I told your father that you might have a little Apache in your belly by now."

She never said another word. He glanced back; with her

slender hand in his grasp, she was keeping up better. He wondered if he had hit a nerve with her with his last statement.

"I know my father never left the hacienda to look for me."

"Why didn't you go home when the Apaches collected the reward?"

"What reward?" she asked as they both rested side by side with their hands on their knees.

"The one he paid them."

"He never paid Tomatoes or his band anything."

"Hmm," he snorted through his nose. "He told me that he paid them and that they refused to give you back." He motioned they must start moving—she obeyed this time without his tug.

"I was waiting in the canyon when the one called Jose, who is a Mexican captive who has lived with them since he was young, rode back and said they had no ransom for me."

"Was Tomatoes mad?" he asked, recovering his saddlebags and rifle.

"I think so, but we just turned our ponies around and went back to the mountains."

"I saw you in the store in Paso."

"You have a nasty habit of spying on me, Señor Slocum." Then she gave a head toss and hurried to keep up with his impatient tugging.

His lungs ached for more air as he wondered about all this. Buck, if he hadn't been discovered, would be on the far side of the moonstruck pine grove. Grateful at last to see his form, Slocum dug out the saddle and pads and carried them to the horse.

He quickly saddled Buck and tied on the bags with the strings. He shoved the rifle in the boot and turned to look at his reluctant companion.

"You going with me?" he asked before he mounted.

"I came this damn far." She looked around in the starlight as if searching for another way or route. "I guess I will," she said, and accepted his arm for a swing up behind.

She settled down on top of his bedroll and put her hands around his waist. "Let's ride, Slocum," she said close to his ear.

Buck picked his way in the dark; they rode until the spears of the new sun crept over the distant peaks. He reined the horse up a side canyon, and then he eased his sleepy passenger to her feet.

"This will be where we rest for a while. If they've started out after us, we still can take a few hours break," he said, dropping heavily to his soles. When he looked around she was gone. He shrugged off her disappearance and waded off the opposite direction to relieve himself.

When he returned she was sipping canteen water. "What do we have to eat?"

"Some jerky."

"Jerky? How much is my father paying you?"

"Two hundred dollars."

"Cheap enough, huh?"

"I guess," he said, taking the canteen. "Last night you didn't really care if you came out of there or not. Why?"

She turned her back to him and looked hard at the sheer face of the canyon wall that towered above them.

"You don't want to talk about it, fine. But I'm getting a couple hours of sleep," he said undoing his blankets. "Here's one for you."

At first she didn't move to accept it. He draped it on her shoulder. He had noticed she wore a collarless blouse and a full skirt with several layers under it: a typical costume of the native Mexican people. She must have lost her fancy clothes somewhere. It was none of his affair, but she was pretty and no doubt spoiled. He dismissed her, went to a place where the pines shaded the ground, and spread out his blanket.

"I'll just be close," she said, and then spread hers down beside him.

He nodded with a whatever look and used his arm for a pillow. He had barely fallen asleep when he heard something and turned to look down the canyon. Horses. Damn if the Apaches weren't already close on their trail. He was on his knees with the Colt in his hand ready.

"Who is it?" she asked in a husky voice.

"I'm not certain. There's a large bunch of riders down there. I first though it was Apaches, but it must be the military."

"Military?"

"Yes, and if they've got scouts, they'll probably find Buck's tracks and come up here. You take him up into the timber and I'll go see who it is."

"What if they capture you?" She looked taken aback at the prospect.

Slocum shrugged away her concern. "You simply ride like hell out of here."

"Oh, that's nice," she said, and ran for the buckskin who grazed on the short grass. Slocum rolled up the blankets and tied them on when she brought the horse to him.

"Go on up there and hide," he said, seeing the impatience in her dark eyes. He drew out the rifle from the boot and the telescope from the packs. Then he headed for the brush to skirt under cover down the canyon to view the large number of horses he could hear.

Finally on his belly, he surveyed the area beyond the mouth of the canyon. His first sight of the red plaid outfit told him enough. McVain's big form on a large black horse told him everything. There were a few of the local Indians telling the big man something. They were his scouts, no doubt. Stray or stupid Indians. Slocum had heard that if McVain's scouts didn't find Apaches to scalp, he took theirs instead.

Close to two dozen riders, Slocum calculated. They showed little interest in Buck's hoofprints. The scouts were indicating south as the way the Apaches had gone.

Out of breath, she dropped down beside him. "Who are they?"

"Look for yourself," he said. "Ain't army, that's for sure."

"McVain!" she gasped. "Those are the bloody scalpers."

"Depends. There are folks that think he's some kind of a god killing those Apaches."

"I detest that butcher. Bloody killers of women and children. We've got to warn Tomatoes!" she said as she clenched her fists at her side.

"How in the hell do you propose to do that?" He couldn't believe his ears. Less than eight hours before, he had rescued her from these same people she wanted to warn.

"The women and children, for them I worry."

He agreed.

"Make a signal fire," she said, as if he should know all about them.

"Yes, and that fat Scot and his scum will be over here on us the minute they see it."

"Do you have a candle?" she asked.

"I might have a stub of one in my saddlebags." What did she want with a candle? He rose to his hands and feet as the riders all appeared to be headed south. Warn the damn Apaches! The poor girl had been out there too long. But he did share her concern for the women and children and what would happen to them in the hands of the scalpers as he gathered dry wood.

At the horse, she grew excited finding the small candle wrapped in oilcloth in his saddlebag.

"You make me a few handfuls of cedar shaving for tinder with your knife and I'll get the dry wood. We'll build it up there." She pointed to a high bare point above them. "Then we simply light the candle. When we're miles away the candle will burn down ignite the cedar and the signal fire will start."

"What if it burns out and doesn't light?"

She looked at him as if puzzled by his negative attitude. "Oh, it always works. Apache squaws do it all the time to make signal fires."

"Fine," he said, and shaved off more slivers from the branch of the sappy pine. It would ignite easily.

"Hurry," she said, and ran off to gather wood for the fire. He paused to observe her furious wood collection. Did she have feelings for this Tomatoes? He kept whittling— no sense ruining her plans to save the Apaches, though he doubted the band would even see the signal.

The great pile of dry wood, with enough green stuff added to cause smoke for the signal, was in place. He handed her a lucifer as she knelt beside the large stack of branches and dead logs they'd dragged up the steep hillside. She struck the match on a rock and carefully put the flame to the candle in the cavern they had created for it in the center. The wick flared and she withdrew the match. A puff of her breath and the match was out.

"Good," she said, pushing herself up. "Let's go."

"That's fire's going to warn him?" he asked, unconvinced.

"McVain won't surprise them," she said flatly.

Slocum shrugged. He closed his dry eyes for a minute, hoped for some tears to wet them, and then opened them again without any moisture. Saving Apaches, not wanting to leave—who was this female he trying to rescue? He offered her a hand to steady her as they came down the steep hillside for the final leg of the trip out of the Madres—he hoped.

8

"Look," she said, pounding on his shoulder as they rode northward.

He turned and saw the first wisps of smoke were rising skyward from the peak far behind them. Yes, her signal fire had worked.

"Think the Apaches will see it in time?" he asked.

"I hope so. I told you before I hate that butcher McVain."

"My next boss you're talking about." Slocum said, and earned himself a hard fist to the kidneys.

"You wouldn't work for that killer, would you, Señor Slocum."

"Might have to to keep from starving to death."

"You can be one of my father's *pistoleros*. He always keeps some at the hacienda."

"What difference is it to kill for your father or kill for McVain?"

"I don't know," she said in the voice of a small girl. "But he does not order his men to kill women and little children and then sell their scalps to the *federales*." She gripped his shoulder and leaned forward to look at him for a reply.

"I don't know about that. How did the Apaches kidnap you anyway?" he asked, his curiosity aroused.

She sat back on the saddle again and did not speak for a long while. Perhaps she couldn't tell him; maybe it was so bad she didn't want to speak of it.

"I am not very good at picking men," she said softly. "See, if I had picked you, instead I would be in Mexico City by now, huh?"

"Who did you pick?"

"This time?" she asked in the small voice.

"Whatever time."

"When I was fourteen, I liked a stable boy named Henry. And one day we made love in the hay. I was so young, he was maybe fifteen. We just started kissing and, oh, soon he was inside me." He felt her straighten herself up behind him.

"And?" Slocum asked, wanting her to continue as he booted Buck into a faster walk. If McVain ever figured out that they had been the ones who warned the Apaches, their lives wouldn't be worth much. He wanted more distance between them and the signal fire.

"Oh, my God, what happened next? Oh, my father sent me to a convent when he found out what I had done."

"How did he find out?"

"I think the main stable man, Jose, told my father. Maybe he watched us do it and then he told him. He was a dirty old man and when he helped me on a horse, his hands stayed too long on me."

"What happened to the boy?"

"Oh, he escaped to Arizona."

"Do you still love him?"

"Oh, that was only puppy love, huh? I told you I was not very good at choosing men."

Slocum looked back. The signal fire was a dark pillar in the sky. He could remember the army wanting the scouts to go capture the ones who set such fires, some green lieutenant sending him and a couple of Apaches to climb a peak and apprehend them. But by the time they scaled it, of course, the fire setters were always gone. Now he knew their secret and the reason the Apache scouts always shook their head about capturing the signal setters.

She hugged his shoulder to shift her butt around on the back of the saddle and be more comfortable.

"Who came next?" he asked over his shoulder.

"Oh, a young *pistolero* called Jerome. But first you must guess how many times they made me do penance and say prayers at the convent for my sin."

"A thousand times?" Slocum laughed.

"A million times I think."

"That must have been some place."

"Yes, but all those other girls in there were dying to hear how I lost my virginity."

"So you told them?"

"I embellished on it!" she said in a deep voice. "Are they ever in for a shock whenever they do it."

"You think they'll be disappointed?" he asked, deep in thought about any possible guards McVain might have left at the narrow ridge crossing.

"More than likely they will be. Are you touching my leg?" She grasped his hand in hers when he reached back.

"No, I want my telescope out of there."

"I'll get it," she said, and moved his hand forward before releasing it. "What is wrong?"

"I want to check this crossing before we go over it. McVain may have it guarded on the other side."

"Oh, you mean the Devil's Backbone. That is what they call it."

"I agree with the name. Let's ride wide of it first just in case. We can go up in the timber, and then I'll get down close and make sure no one is on either end."

They left Buck in the timber and slipped down hill to a great flat rock, a perfect place to spy from. When they bellied down side by side on their elbows, he could not see anything or anyone on their side of the bridge.

"Well?" she asked as he adjusted the focus of the telescope and peered in the lens.

"Damn," he swore as he handed her the glass. Three men with an obvious purpose were squatted around a small fire, drinking coffee on the far side of the narrow trail through the sky.

"There are only three of them," she said with a know-it-all grin.

"Beyond rifle range too. I'm not going out there and get shot off my horse in the middle of nowhere. We'll have to ride on." Disappointed that they were within a half day's ride of Paso and couldn't use the route, he took the brass telescope back and collapsed it.

"I've never been north of this point," she said, rolling over on her back and looking up at the sky.

"I guess you will today." He said, glancing over at her. She certainly had a good figure.

"I guess I will. Slocum, are you like those princes that I read about that rescue fair damsels from castles?"

"No, I'm the guy who rescues non-virgins from Apaches."

She hit him in the arm with her fist. Her full lips pursed tight together, she drew back to hit him again. "You're making fun of me."

"I'd never do that," he said smugly, and raised up. What ever was in those mountains ahead, they would soon find out. "Let's ride."

"We could get lost up here and never get out."

"I've been lost before and always found a way out. I guess if your reputation can stand a few more days—" He ducked as she tried to slap him with both hands.

"I won't ever tell you another thing. Not one more thing! Do you hear me?"

"Quiet or McVain's guards might hear you."

She frowned in their direction and wrinkled her nose. "I hate them too."

"Get up here, girl," he said, already mounted, as he hoisted her up by the arm. "We ain't got time for that, we've got miles to ride."

"I hate you too," she pouted as she adjusted her balance behind him.

"It comes in spells is all." He laughed as he reined Buck off the slope and into the dark timber. Somewhere there was another way out of these mountains. Not an easy one either or else no one but a fool would ever use the Devil's Crossing.

"Let's see," Slocum began as the exaggerated steps of Buck going downhill threw her against him. Her hard breasts buried in his back, and a small smile formed in the corner of his mouth—there had been worse jobs than this one.

They slept in their own blankets without a fire, beside a small stream that rushed headlong down its course. Enough grass close by for Buck.

In the early light, he watched her out of slitted eyes as she went to the stream, undressed, and with her shapely back to him, sat down in the water and bathed herself with small outcries about the coldness.

He finally rose and went off in the woods to relieve himself. When he returned she had dressed and rolled up their blankets, and waited for him.

"More jerky?" She held out her hand.

"We're nearly out of that," he said, looking around. "I don't dare shoot a gun either. Might wake up some other Apaches."

"Oh, jerky isn't bad," she said, taking the flat piece he handed her. She chewed on it with great effort.

"Sorry. I guess you're used to fancy breakfasts. Maybe blackberries in Jersey cream, huh?"

"What are they?" she asked, looking sideways at him.

"I guess they don't grow down here," he said.

"Fruit? huh?"

"Yes, they grow on thorny bushes. When they are ripe and about the size of your thumb, they're sure good to eat. They grow all over the Southern states."

"It rains a lot up there?"

"More than down here."

"It is going to rain here soon," she said, looking up at the cloudless azure sky.

"How do you know that?" He looked over at her as he squatted on the ground close by her seat on a large rock.

"I heard an owl hoot three times in the daytime."

"Must not have been a Mexican owl."

"We'll see. Excuse me, sir," she said, and rose to her feet. With a small bow she left him and walked off out of sight behind some willowy growth. He went to ready the horse. They had another day's ride ahead.

By late afternoon, the thunderstorms that she promised had swept over the mountains and soaked both of them to the skin. He headed Buck down a steep slope on a dim path. Maybe it was an old game trail that they followed. He only knew they were still moving northward when he spotted a cave on the slope above them and pointed it out to her.

"We might dry up there," he said.

"Good, let's go. I'm freezing."

He could feel her shivering behind him. "Might be a bear den," he said over his shoulder.

"Me afraid of a bear? Why, I'll just have my own personal *pistolero* shoot it."

"Hope that sumbitch comes quick if there's a bear."

She poked him hard in the back, as she did often to make her points. "I meant you."

"Oh."

He unsaddled Buck a hundred feet beneath the cave's mouth, and was forced to climb over a great slab that fell from above cave's mouth onto the hillside making a sheer face to clamber over. Finally across it, he checked to be sure she was coming. Her wet hair plastered to her face, she scrambled with great effort over the steep rock on hands and knees. Satisfied she was making it, he carried the saddle and gear up the steep rocky path along the face of the mountain. She came behind.

Out of breath, he was glad to see the dry dirt under the overhang. From the soot-coated ceiling he concluded that others over the years had used this place for the same purpose. He searched around and saw no fresh animal signs, no bones, parts of hide or game parts half-eaten that would indicate a lair. Satisfied it was safe enough to leave her, he turned his thoughts to his horse's care.

"You stay here. I'm taking Buck down where he can find something to eat."

She hugged her arms and shivered. Her teeth even clicked, she was so cold. "I'll be here when you get back, I guess."

"Get under a blanket. Even wet they'll beat nothing."

"Go on, I'll be fine." She shooed him away.

Further down the mountainside, he found Buck some feed and left him on the rope to graze. With great effort, Slocum climbed back up to the steep path with an armload of dead wood he'd gathered.

He dumped the load unceremoniously at her feet. She had found the blanket and huddled under it.

"I'm better," she said, and he headed out again to find more fuel. It would be hard to start, but he found some twisted juniper, and it would burn hot once he got it going. More thunder heralded the approach of another shower as he searched about, loading his arms with more deadwood.

Finally he had the fire blazing in their shelter; the heavy curtain of rain at the mouth of the cave had shut out any view they had. The crackling fire's heat felt good and drove much of the cold from him as she sat tucked under his arm like a baby chicken.

"You get warm enough, we'll spread those blankets out and dry them," he said.

"I may never get warm again." She wrapped herself tighter in the covers.

He was about to agree with her when he blinked in disbelief as a tall figure in rainslick buckskins stepped through the rain curtain and leveled a Winchester at him.

"Ah, señor, put your hands high!" the man said, motioning with his gun barrel. He wore a four-peak sombrero and spoke from behind a black beard. But the set in his dark coal eyes told Slocum all he needed to know—this hombre was tough. "Come in, amigos, I have this big one covered."

Slocum sized his chances with his arms raised—none at the moment. Who the hell was the man and his amigos? Thunder across the range rumbled as the other two wet outlaws joined him.

9

His head still rang from where they had slugged him with the rifle butt from behind his back. Without moving his cheek on the gritty surface, he barely cracked open his right eye to locate them. The dirt in his mouth, he decided, came from the cave floor under his cheek. He spotted the leader. He dared not spit out the bitter dirt or even show a sign of life.

The main one was a hardcase they called Honcho. The two boys who came with him looked like they were fresh from some isolated village. Both acted inexperienced at this outlaw game they played. The youths did things hesitantly; timid enough that if he could eliminate this Honcho character, then he doubted they would fight long.

His situation was not good, and he wondered about Lucia as he discovered his hands were tied up in front. They were bound tight enough that the cord cut deep into his wrists; he lay on the hard ground grateful that they had not tied his legs. Had they tried to bind up his feet, no doubt they would have found his knife and the derringer in his other boot.

"So Señorita Sallisar, this big gringo, he rescues you from the Apaches?" Honcho was cleaning his teeth with a fresh sliver of wood he had whittled off a branch from the firewood pile.

"My father will pay you well for my safe return," she said, sitting very demurely on a large flat rock formation.

"You think he wants the gringo alive too, huh?"

"I think he would pay you well for him. He is his best *pistolero*."

Honcho held his toothpick away from his mouth. "I think he would say good riddance of that gringo bastard. Now he don't have to pay him no damn reward."

"Oh, no, he is an employee of the hacienda."

"He may never wake up from that blow I give him."

"Can I see about him?"

"No," Honcho said, reaching out and captured her chin in his hand. "I may make you my woman. Why did he bring you this way? The Devil's Crossing is the only way down there."

"We ah—"

"Ah, I know what you are doing. This big gringo and you were going to run away together, no?"

"No."

"You lie, little one." He dragged her to her feet by the hold on her face and pulled her close to his mouth. "I will have your body; then if the Don wants to buy you back, he can have the used merchandise."

"He will be mad if you damage it," she warned. Her words were slurred by his grip on her jaw.

"You will be more valuable when I am done with you, for then you will know how to pleasure a man."

There wasn't much time. Slocum could see this outlaw was about to get worked up. Where were those boys? He could not hear them. They might jump in and try to save their boss no matter how slow they acted otherwise.

He only had one option, somehow to reach down and get the derringer out of his boot and fire point-blank at him. A bolt of lightning struck so close the flash blinded him for a second and the crash was so loud it hurt his ears. Rain in sheets blocked the cave entrance as another downpour gained momentum. He could feel a fine spray from the downpour on his face. Another blast of thunder—

"Let me see your tits!" The sound of the material being

torn and her cry of distress brought him to action. His hands dove into his boot tops and came out with the double-barrel derringer in his grasp. He touched the floor with the heel of his gun hands to gain his feet, then rushed across the cave to where Honcho stood staring down at her exposed breasts.

"Honcho!" he shouted, and the man whirled to face him.

Both barrels fired and caused the small pistol to nearly jump out of his grasp. The outlaw staggered back, crying, "You've killed me!"

"Get his gun!" Slocum shouted to Lucia, and whirled, pointing the smoking gun at the other two outlaws.

His action was too much for the pair of boys. Slocum could read their fear through the cloud of gunsmoke veiling the cavern. Wide-eyed, desperate to save their own skins, and not aware that the derringer he held was empty, they both rushed out the cave entrance without thinking about the sheer dropoff and fell screaming to the rocks below.

"My knife is in my boot," he said to her, holding out his hands for her to cut them free. The youths' cries of fear faded in the thrash of the rain outside.

With a confident smile on her face, she jammed Honcho's pistol in his waistband and knelt down to draw out the Bowie knife as he watched the wounded outlaw lying on his back. His buckskin shirtfront was bathed in blood. Some black powder still smoldered on the man's chest, which he tried to put out, burning his palms.

"Oh," Honcho cried, looking down, fear-filled, at his wound, "I am dying. You have killed me."

Lucia hurriedly sawed on the ropes that bound Slocum's wrists, parting the cords one at a time. Finally free, he recovered his own gun from a pile and covered the outlaw as he advanced toward him.

"Lucia, gather up all their guns. Those other two are gone. I doubt they will be back."

"What about him?" she asked, holding her torn blouse together with one hand. "Will he die?"

"Honcho?" Slocum asked with a smug grin.

She frowned at him and shook her head, not understanding his amusement.

"Someone will kill him some day, but I haven't. The little gun was only loaded with rock salt, peppercorn, and black powder. It will burn like hell, but I never knew of the mixture killing anyone. I think it was Doc Holiday, in Ft Worth. One time he caught a guy cheating and shot him under the table with the same mixture. They say the guy ran out the door and sat in a watering tank, but that only made it worse."

"Rock salt, is that what's burning me so bad?" Honcho asked with great effort, inspecting his chest.

Slocum gave the man a kick to get his attention. "Who do you work for?"

"No one."

"Are you scouting for McVain?"

"Not anymore," he said with discomfort written on his whiskered face as he sat up.

"What are you doing up here anyway?"

"Sometimes you can find small camps of Apaches."

"Women and children?"

"No, no—I never take them" He looked up with dread at Lucia and then at Slocum.

"I wish you'd had a real bullet in your gun," she said to Slocum, and then she kicked Honcho hard in the other leg. "You no-good bastard you were going to rape me too, weren't you?"

"No, señorita." He put his arms over his head as she flailed him with her fists.

"Here, here, save your strength," Slocum said, pulling her away from him.

Her rage was out of control, and her full lip stuck out taut as a bowstring as Slocum held her arm and drew her up on her toes to stop her from hitting the man. Both her exposed dollar-sized nipples turned rock hard to match her diamond eyes that flashed with revenge.

To handle her better as they struggled, he holstered his Colt. There was simply no sense letting her do something she would regret later. Finally he held her by her upper arms, hoisted on her toes close to his chest, until he was satisfied most of her fire had been extinguished. Then slowly he lowered her to the ground, looking hard into her eyes. They stood for a long moment staring at each other and feeling the power of two strong-willed people only inches apart.

"We better tie him up," Slocum said to break the impasse. "It will be a long time until sunup."

"Yes," she said softly, and went for the rest of the rope the outlaws had brought into the cave to tie him up with.

10

The rain passed in the night. It cleansed the air and the skies were a new blue as Slocum hurried over the wet trail in search of his horse. Water dripped off the pine needles in small showers on him soaking into his shirt. He wondered how much further they must ride before they would find an outlet out of the Madres. It was time that they found one and were on their way to her father's hacienda. Another day's ride north and they would be near the Rio Blanco and Natise's country—he was not anxious to tangle with Cochise's son again. Next time the chieftain was likely to forget that Slocum ever knew his father.

Buck raised his head and nickered to him. Close by another horse grazed, a bay that showed saddle scars. Slocum's hand touched his Colt handle as he searched around. It could be Honcho's horse or it might be a trap. He'd not seen nor heard any more from the two boys who'd jumped out of the cave. Perhaps he had taught them a lesson about why they should not join up with some big-talking outlaw like Honcho. Here there was no sign of anything.

He captured the bay and led the two horses back to the foot of the cave trail. He decided Lucia could ride Buck, for he was sure-footed and the new horse's ability was unknown. He would use their gear and ride the bay.

"What about him?" she asked, concerned about the

bound-up outlaw in the cave as they prepared to ride on.

"You can't leave me here to starve, hombre," Honcho said.

"Honcho, as low-life as you are, I could leave you for the red ants to eat," Slocum said.

"You won't do that, would you, señor? Please, in the name of God?"

"I'll cut your feet loose," Slocum said, finally relenting at her concerned look. "Then you can get your hands loose somehow after we leave. But if you follow us, you're dead. Savvy?"

"Oh, I swear. You will never see me again."

"If I do, I won't use rock salt on your hide." Slocum cut the binds on the man's legs as he sat on the cave floor with his hands tied behind him.

They rode north. On the trail he spotted signs of the other two horses' tracks where they had fled the night before. He and Lucia rode single-file with him in the lead, keeping an eye on the slopes above and what lie ahead. When he looked back he noted that she had mended her torn blouse, and appeared to be studying the forests as they rode under a great rock escarpment that towered above them. Water- and wind-gnarled red rock cliffs made a sheer face rising several hundred feet above the talus rock at the base.

"Don't look up now," he said, "but we've got company."

She pushed Buck in close. "Who is it?"

"A half-dozen braves are up there on horses."

"You've seen them?"

"Yes, there, you can hear their ponies." He turned an ear to listen for the sound of hoofbeats on rocks again.

"What will we do?"

"Unless they find a way down they aren't much threat."

"But what will we do if they come down."

"Ride like hell, I guess." He shrugged and sent the bay into a faster walk.

"You said you didn't know this country."

"I don't, but that bluff they're on goes for miles and I don't see a break in it, do you?"

"No, but—"

"Odds are, they can't come down here any easier than we can find a way west to get down off these mountains, so we're at a standoff."

She looked up and made a face at the scene above them. "I'm ready to get out of here."

"We will," Slocum promised as he saw the five riders on their horses high above gather for a conference. He made a big wave and let out a kii-yiing cry for their sake.

"Quit tempting them," she hissed.

Slocum chuckled at her words. Hell, they were too far away to get a rifle shot off and hit a damn thing. Still, he had to admit she was tough enough for a rich girl raised in a big house with all the spoils of the very well-to-do.

"Tell me about your affair with the *pistolero*," he said over his shoulder.

"And have those bucks up there hear it too, I suppose?" she demanded.

"They couldn't hear nothing," he said, watching a pair of vultures swoop down off the rim and circle, expectantly searching in flight.

"I'm not telling you another thing."

"Aw, come on. You ran off with him?"

"I was in love with him is the only reason."

"Jerome is the one?" He turned in the saddle to look at her and check their backtrail.

"After yesterday, I shouldn't even tell you a thing—he was a very pretty young man. Dark eyes and very small butt. I had watched him dance. And, well, I decided he would be very exciting."

"More exciting than a stable boy."

"No comparison, so I began to meet him in dark places."

"Barns?"

"No, once a fool, I learned about men. I only met him in the hallways, we stole kisses. I recalled very well how easy haystacks became a bed for lovers. See, I planned our meetings and we only had a few minutes each time. Then there would be footsteps on the tile and we would separate. It was exciting and he breathed fire for me.''

"I bet he did.'' Slocum saw the bucks high above them lined out single-file in the timber. The party must have decided to parallel their route until they had perhaps had a chance to descend on them.

"They aren't going to get down here, are they?'' she asked in a small girl's voice.

"No.'' He dismissed her fears with a wave of his hand. "So you ran off with him.''

"He promised to take me to the priest in San Raye and we would be married.''

"So you eloped with him.''

"Yes. I climbed out my window on a ladder that he brought to the wall. He waited below with two horses from my father's stables. It was a dark night. Once on the ground, he kissed me so deep I could hardly find my breath. Then he helped me on my mount. Very romantic. I knew at last I had found a great man for the rest of my life.''

"You married him?''

"No, the priest at San Raye told him he could not do it without my father's approval.''

"So you went home?''

"Oh, no, I should have, but I was so mad that we rode off to Mexico City anyway.''

"Like you two had been married.''

"Yes,'' she sighed deeply. "We stopped at a small empty *jacale* and spread on the floor the fine blankets I had taken from my room. But then things became worse; my groom was unable to do anything. His thing would not work and he became very abusive, blaming me.''

"Some honeymoon you had,'' he said. Unable to see the Apaches, he rose in the stirrups and searched the top of the rim for a sign of them.

"I began to think I was his problem,'' she said, obviously not aware of Slocum's newfound concern. "But for three days he tried many times to use his small prod and it would not go in me.''

"What happened next?'' The hostiles still were not in

his sight, and Slocum began to wonder if they had found a way down or had simply split off abandoning the notion of capturing them.

"He simply rode off and left me there."

"He left you out there in nowhere?" Slocum could hardly believe her words.

"Yes, I think he had become convinced that my father would hang him for stealing horses and taking his daughter against the expressed order of a priest too. But you can guess who rode up while I was stomping and cussing that whinny little steer for leaving me out there afoot?"

"The Apaches?" he asked, itching to do something about being on the mountain.

"Yes."

"Save the rest," he said. "I want to hear all about it later, but I think we better try to go down this slope and see if we can get out of these mountains."

"You think those Apaches are coming down?" She tossed her head in their direction.

"Right," he said, and reined the bay straight down the mountainside. Loose talus scattered under the bay's feet as Slocum turned and shouted for her to give Buck his head. The bay horse's ears went out of sight as he scrambled and skidded down the steep hillside of flat loose rock. Leaning back until the cantle cut into his back, Slocum hoped he saw a flat at the base where they could regroup on.

At her shout, he managed to twist and see Buck recover and plunge downward with her nearly jerked from the saddle; only her grip on the horn had saved her and the last he saw, she had recovered. His bay slid the last few hundred feet on his hooves, but finally landed on the solid base. Trembling under the saddle, the horse shook with all his might as the palefaced Lucia joined him on the snorting buckskin.

She cast a wary look up the slope. "That was a helluva way to come down."

With no time to waste, he booted the bay down the game trail that filed close to the canyon wall. "We ain't got the time to talk. Come on."

"Yes, sir!" And she put Buck in after him.

The narrow route wound around the face of the layered cliff, and he could see a hundred miles of rolling desert far below to the west from their slender perch on the mountain face. He worried the trail might belong to the desert sheep instead of being one that led to some water source lower down, as most game trails eventually did. The desert sheep only went to places where they could escape a coyote or red wolf by tiptoeing away on some edge too narrow for the predator or for Slocum's bay.

"What if we fall off here?" she asked in her little-girl voice.

"I won't get your father's reward."

"Mother of God, I hope you collect it twice."

"Yes, I hope so too," he said as the trail switched back to cut steeply downward without much ahead that he could see to ride upon.

Then another steep section appeared, and he shifted easy like to look back up the mountain at their back trail. No sign of the Apaches, but that was not to say that they might not be coming. His gut was drawn up considerably by the lack of food, but more by the tight fit the horses had to follow to keep from falling a couple of thousand feet to their death. It was no place for either of them to stumble.

"Gawdamnit, Slocum! We aren't eagles," she swore as the wind began to pick up and batter them.

"Hush and don't look down. We can't go back."

"I know that."

Below them he could see some ranch headquarters that appeared to be smaller than the heads of the matches in his vest. His mouth watered for something to smoke, but he had enjoyed the last quarlie over a day before. It would teach him to buy more next time. Then the bay jammed his left stirrup into the rock wall and forced Slocum to lift up his boot as high as the swell on that side.

The horse stopped and lowered his head to see where to step next; the rounded rock before him looked slick. There was no place to dismount, and Slocum had no choice but to lift the reins to signal the bay to try it.

The first step his hoof slid precariously, and Slocum's heart stopped—she was ready to try and dismount where there was no place but air to step—but the hoof finally caught and the horse quickly placed the other beside it, then made a hop forward with his two hind feet that caught Slocum's breath.

The bay settled with four hooves close together on a precious piece of real estate for a long moment. Then with his head low, he moved forward on the path that went downhill.

Slocum didn't even look back when Lucia gave a cry of fright crossing the same place. But he closed his eyes and nodded to himself when he heard the reassuring sound of Buck's shod hooves on the rock; then he resumed his hard breathing.

The trail widened and he stretched his tight muscles, but his inside boot still scuffed on the wall that rose above them. It was another hour of slow treading before they reached the palm-choked canyon floor.

He dismounted and swept off his hat to mop his sweaty forehead when the horse reached the flat ground. One more time the Great Spirit had helped him over a place where angels would have feared to tread—thanks. He let the snorting bay loose to go for a drink from the small stream that coursed through the canyon. Then he replaced his hat and took Lucia in his arms to help her off Buck. Neither said a word, as they tried to gather their senses. Too weak to stand on her own, she clung to him like a doll.

"Are you planning to rest here?" she asked.

"For a while. Why?"

"I have to clean myself up," she mumbled as she stood by herself.

"Clean up for what?" he asked, wondering who was there but the two of them.

"Thanks to your eagle flight down that mountain, I have peed all over myself."

His face fast heating up to red, he picked up Buck's rein. "Take all the time you need."

11

They rode up to the hacienda's main gate and were halted by guards dressed in gold braided vests and wearing bandoliers. In Slocum's opinion, these men appeared to make up a very impressive defense force that minded the main road going into the vast acreage. Earlier, she had explained that they would cross Sallisar's holdings for miles. The farmland was watered by artesian wells. The guards, upon discovering who she was, all quickly removed their great Chiluhuhua sombreros and bowed to her.

"And this man is with me," she said loud enough that they all nodded they had heard her. With that she rode on. Slocum gave them a salute and followed her through the gates.

Workers in the fields swept off their hats for her passing, and shouted how glad they were to see her alive and safe.

She smiled and rode the buckskin horse like a princess. Even Buck acted as if he knew it was time to show off, and single-footed sideways for her. Slocum scrubbed his beard stubble with his palm, and wished he had swung by Santa Cristo and found her some new clothes. It made no difference. She still looked like royalty in her tattered outfit.

An old man driving a cart and two-ox team shouted jubilantly at the sight of her. This daughter was obviously a favorite of the hacienda people. He even began to feel a little better about his returning her, though there were many things unanswered that he wondered about.

"Did you pick a man among the Apaches?" he asked, pushing the bay in close.

She waved at some young children lining the road to wave at her. "Do you know the Apache Tomatoes?"

"No."

"He is a handsome man."

"And?"

"I was a woman," she said, under her breath, "who had been broken and felt I was of no use to any man."

"And?"

"You can guess the rest. It was better with him than I had told the girls in the convents it would be."

"So that is why you hesitated about leaving his camp?"

She nodded, and waved back at the two men busy irrigating the knee-high corn. The silver ribbons of liquid inched down between the ridges bearing the plants.

"I would have stayed, but he has a wife at San Carlos."

"Oh, I see." Slocum guided the bay aside for a wagon of hay to pass.

"No, you don't!" She pushed Buck in close to speak in a hard hiss. "He said he'd divorced her because she would not leave the reservation with him."

"Your religion? Him being divorced was why you didn't become his wife?"

"Not really. Men have lied to me before. Do you understand? Could I believe him that he had divorced her?"

"I don't know either."

"I was not going to be another of his wives, understand?"

Slocum indicated he understood. "About the reward that your father paid them, was that a trick?"

She shrugged and looked at him questioningly. "The Apaches never got it. My father was very angry at me for running away with Jerome. Maybe he only said he paid it."

"He has lots of hired men on this place. Why didn't he send his *pistoleros* after you?"

"Maybe he wanted to be rid of me." She smiled and greeted some *vaqueros* who came up the road riding three abreast. They removed their hats and yipped a welcome for her, and shouted how pleased they were that she was back safe.

Slocum let them ride on before he spoke again. "He said your mother cries each day for you."

"Hmm. He hardly cares what she does."

"One thing we can do is ask him all about it."

"You will stay with me?" she asked with a serious, pleading look.

He frowned at her. "I'm not your—"

"Lover?" She laughed aloud and then turned her face away embarrassed. They rode a distance before she spoke to him again.

"Slocum, I meant for you to stay as a guest at the hacienda for a while." She booted Buck in close and touched his arm. "I don't intend to be locked away in a convent. Promise me that you won't let them do that to me?"

"How can I promise you that?" He shook his head at her impossible request.

"Anyone who could sneak up on Apaches and steal me away from them can do anything. You can take me to El Paso del Norte and I'll be a *puta* there, but I will kill myself if they lock me up in a convent."

"Why would they do that?"

"For shaming him by running off with a man. Promise me?"

"You have my word."

"I owe you, big man." She rode close again and clapped him on the leg. "Now you can tell me about this woman in Cristo."

He looked at her sharply. "The witch? How do you know about her?"

"Women have their ways." She wrinkled her nose. "You have plans for her?"

"No one has plans for her. She is like smoke. Sometimes she smothers me, then she is gone as fast on another wind."

"She must be a powerful one."

"She is, because she called me back here, I guess," he said, looking across the orderly vineyards of Sallisar. They were heavy with small green fruit in great bunches. "I guess, to find you. Maybe you are the witch." He slapped the saddlehorn and shook his head. "I should have known that was why they didn't tie you up."

"Why is that?" She shot him a hard look.

"Tomatoes knew your powers and did not wish to have the wraith of a witch upon him."

"Tomatoes?"

"Yes. Will you return to him?"

"No, he is still married to the woman in the north. I would not share a man," she said in the little-girl voice. "You just remember your promise to me, amigo."

"I will."

Don Sallisar welcomed his daughter with open arms. His wife, dressed in black and in tears, rushed into the yard and hugged her daughter. She was an attractive woman, and her daughter was a copy of her mother's beauty. Thickset with middle age, the woman still showed her elegance when she came over and offered her hand to Slocum. Hat in hand, feeling out of place and dirty, Slocum took it and kissed it.

"I don't know what my husband has promised you in the way of money, but it would never be enough. Here, I wish you to have this ring as my token of appreciation." She twisted it free from her finger, a gold band studded with rubies, and placed it in his hand. "It is but a token of my great thanks to you, sir, for bringing my lovely Lucia back."

"Slocum's the name ma'am. But I could never wear such a ring."

"Take it anyway, Slocum. It costs hundreds, I think." She pressed the circle into his hand and closed his fingers on it.

"Thank you," he said as she rushed off to her daughter. They went to the house, both talking at the same time and leaning on each other.

"As you can see, my wife not only was very distressed by her daughter's absence, but she was so shaken by her return, she mistakenly gave you a very valuable ring."

Slocum nodded and considered the man's words. He would have handed back the jewelry a moment before the man spoke, but the tone of the Don's words made him change his mind. "I believe we agreed to two hundred American in gold, sir."

"I stand here and can't believe my ears—why, that ring is—"

"That was a gift, sir, from a lady that I fear that you don't deserve. You can pay me now what you owe me." He looked hard at the ring in the sunlight as the red facets gleamed rays of light, then pocketed it in his vest.

Sallisar's face clouded with his growing impatience. "Slocum, I can have you shot before you get off my lands."

"You saying you won't pay me the money you promised for the safe return of your daughter?"

"I say, sir, you have stolen that ring. I demand its return."

Something snapped inside his head. Slocum heard a dozen rifles click, perhaps only in his imagination, but he was in this man's fiefdom. The itching on the back of his neck was warning enough. He took hold of the saddlehorn in both hands and bounded up in the saddle.

"Sallisar, there will be another day." He reined Buck around sharply. "Remember, I took her away from Apaches. You are a stupid knave compared to them. But I can tell you one thing, you cheap sumbitch. I intend to nail your hide to the barn wall for not paying me my small bill."

"I will see you in jail."

"You intend to have a warrant out for me?" There was no sign of Lucia or her mother, only the big house and the huge olive trees swaying like dancers in the wind.

"Yes, for robbery. The theft of one gold ring with rubies that belongs to my wife."

"I know now that you never paid that ransom to the

Apaches either, did you?'' How could this man be so stingy to risk his own daughter's life?

''I would have. I had a barrel of whiskey for them laced with strychnine.'' Sallisar grinned so smugly that Slocum wanted to kick him in the face with his boot toe.

''Don't close your eyes when you sleep, Don Sallisar. Hee Yah, Buck!'' he shouted, putting his heels to the horse's side, and barely avoided colliding with Sallisar, who only saved himself by diving to the side. The bay spooked with him and raced beside the buckskin. They swept out the yard gate and down the road. Their manes in the wind, Slocum charged northward, scattering shocked peons from the roadway in his wake.

Then Slocum reined in the buckskin. There was no sign of anyone on his backtrail yet. No doubt the man's *pistoleros* were still busy saddling. But he knew that he would never live to ride out through the main north gate. Sallisar would already have orders sent there for the guards to shoot him on sight.

He turned Buck aside. The buckskin easily cleared the ditch filled with water and with the bay beside him, raced over the close-clipped alfalfa stubble. Next, screaming like an Apache in case some one was working in the rows, he raced through a quarter-mile-long row of grapes. The leaves, vines, and green grapes all beating his legs, he emerged on the third field road and drew Buck alongside the bay so he could switch places without dismounting.

Free of his weight the buckskin fell in beside his mount, matching the bay's stride. Both horses were lathered after the near-mile run, but they ran unfazed and the desert was less than a half mile ahead. In those dry washes and mesquite thickets ahead, he felt confident, he could lose all but a Yaqui tracker.

Damn—he lay on the bay's neck and let the horses run. No sign of anyone, but they would come.

12

"You mean he refused to pay you?" Estrallia sounded as exasperated as Slocum had been hours earlier during his confrontation at the hacienda with Don Sallisar.

"This man had both of us fooled. Completely fooled," he said, seated at the small wooden table, busy eating her food.

"But everyone on the hacienda loves her. She always has time for them. My cousin Lupe was so distressed about the Apaches taking her that she begged me to help her father."

"She eloped with a boy who got afraid and abandoned her. That is how the Apaches captured her."

Estrallia shook her head and looked at him distressed. "Oh, I see. There was nothing said about that."

"Now her father will probably ship her off to a convent."

"That is not so unusual in this land. Many fathers encourage their daughters to wed Christ."

He pointed a spoon at her. "Perhaps so, but she considered it imprisonment and I gave my word to her, I wouldn't let him lock her up in a convent."

"How could you do such a thing?" She frowned in disbelief at him.

"Do such a thing? By gawd, she asked me to promise

her that I would not let them lock her up in one.''

"But—"

"Estrallia, you've got relatives that work on that hacienda. I want word the minute he plans to do that to her. I figure he will let her stay with her mother a few days, maybe a week. Then I feel certain that he will ship her out. It will be hard to learn when, unless there is someone on the inside who will find out for you.''

She shook her head as if peeved with him. "Did this girl mesmerize you or something in the mountains?''

"Yes, she did. You can find out for me?''

"Yes, my cousin Lupe works in the main house. I will send her word today that I need to know. She will tell me when anything is about to happen.'' Estrallia slipped into his lap and forced him to eat around her as she nestled on his chest. "Enough talking about this matter. I have worried about you for many days.''

"Yes, well, I had—" She silenced him with a kiss. Her arms encircled his neck and she drove her firm breasts into his chest. He closed his eyes to savor her closeness.

"I'm unshaven, road-dirty, and smell like a horse,'' he protested in her ear, but she ignored his concern instead she pushed back his vest, then carefully undid the shirt buttons until it fell open. She ran her palms over his muscle-corded belly and then massaged his back. Snakelike with her fingernail, she traced the tract of black hair that ran down the center of his chest to his belt.

"Who cares? I want you.'' She dismissed any concern about his condition.

"I damn sure don't.''

He toed off his boots as he kissed her; finally their mouths became so compressed, he saw stars. Their clothes flew away like dirt from a new gopher hole, until he found himself sprawled on top of her ripe form in the small bed. Her legs spread apart for his entry; she bit his shoulder in delight as he gained her gates.

The ropes under the cot protested their movements. Her sleeping cats, awakened by their unbridled passion, fled the room in shock; one in its haste dislodged a pot that broke on the floor in a shattering crash that distracted Estrallia for a minute, but he reassured her he'd buy her a dozen more. Without another word, they resumed their unbridled love-making in earnest until both were spent, and then they fell asleep.

"Señora! Señora!" Someone rapped urgently on the door.

He raised up, realizing she had gotten up and no longer nestled under his arm, as he tried to open his eyes and watch her dress. She slipped into a robe to wrap her nakedness and went to answer the door; he listened to the soft voices in the hallway.

She rushed in the room wrapping herself in the robe and obviously upset. "Maria, my friend, she said the *federales* are coming to arrest you. They are a few hours away."

"Damn Sallisar anyway," he said, running his fingers through his hair. "I'll go up and try to stay with my friend Goldfarb at Paso. You listen for any news about Lucia and send me word up there."

"You really think Don Sallisar would do such a thing to a girl that is so loved by the people on the hacienda?"

"He's so proud he can't stand that."

Estrallia narrowed her eyes in disbelief at his words. "But he has no heirs except her. At least she could give him a grandson to inherit his hacienda."

"She does not pick men from high enough stations to suit him."

Estrallia shot a hard look at him. "What men does she choose?"

"She chose a young *pistolero* to elope with. He became afraid and left her to be kidnapped by the Apaches and Tomatoes."

"Tomatoes?" She frowned as he busied himself dressing.

"It is a nickname, a tag they gave him because he likes the canned ones so much." He stomped on his boots, then rubbed his beard cheek; there was no time for a shave. At Paso, he would get one.

He buckled on his six-gun and patted the first cat, who balanced himself on the slender arm of the chair purring for his attention. "Sure could have used your agility when we came off those mountains." He laughed to himself about the notion of riding a cat down those slopes.

"Those scalp hunters haven't been back, have they?" he asked.

"No."

"Then I better hurry and warn Goldfarb that they're planning a trap."

"Who, the *federales*?" Estrallia asked, returning with a clean shirt for him to take with him. "At times you speak in riddles."

"McVain and his scalpers. I have no time to explain. Here, this is for you." He dug the ring out of his vest pocket and gave it to her. "Sallisar's wife gave it to me for bringing the girl in. He demanded it back and this is what he's accusing me of stealing from him."

"Oh, it is too valuable. I could never wear it." Her brown lips formed an O as she admired the sparkling ring pinched between her fingertips.

"When this is all over I want you to wear it. It is like a beautiful painting, but it is no good unless people can see it," he said, and slapped on his hat.

Her arms quickly enclosed his neck and she rose on her toes, pressing her ripe form into him, dragging his mouth close to hers. "Would you think of me as a *puta* if I accept it?"

"Never." He looked deep into her eyes, and then he kissed her good-bye.

Paso looked unchanged; the afternoon wind scattered the cooking fires' smoke below Buck's knees as Slocum rode up the street. Children ran about, yelling in shrill voices, as he dismounted in front of the store.

"Ah, the man is back. You may be a ghost," Goldfarb said, standing in the doorway. "Did you get the girl already?"

Slocum nodded and gazed about the small village. Satisfied no threat existed, he turned back and nodded to his friend. "She's been home several days now."

"My God, man, you are a magician."

"I could say I planned it all." He smiled, amused at his host's praise.

"Come inside, I'll find you a good cigar and we can drink some rye and you can tell me how one extracts a hostage from the Apaches."

"Like pulling the fangs out of a rattler—careful like."

"I believe that. Ruby, look who is back and the Sallisar girl is at home. Can you believe that?"

"She is safe?" Ruby asked, blinking in disbelief.

"Didn't you notice that she was safe even when she was here with the Apaches?" Slocum said.

"What do you mean?" the woman asked.

"Couldn't you see the air about her when she came in the store?"

"No."

"She has magic powers."

"You believe in magical powers?" she asked.

"Yes, I believe some women especially have powers. They can know things that are happening many miles away. They can even summon help and sometimes curse others."

"This woman has such powers?" Ruby asked.

"She has some of them," Slocum said as he sniffed the length of the fine cigar his host had chosen for him.

"Come upstairs, business is slow enough," Goldfarb said as Slocum snipped the end off the cigar with his jackknife and wet the long tube with the tip of his tongue.

"Great," he said as he took the stairs ahead of his host.

"Ruby, send up some food," Goldfarb said.

They lounged on the balcony, sipping rye, and when she brought the food tray, they enjoyed mesquite-flavored goat. Roasted a golden brown, the spicy, tender chevron melted in his mouth. Slocum wiped his greasy fingers on a towel Ruby had provided, and then mopped his mouth after licking his slick lips for the last of the tangy flavor.

"So the *federales* now want you?" Goldfarb said, sitting

back and folding his hands over his ponderous bulk.

"For stealing a ring his wife gave me as a reward. It is a damn sight cheaper than paying me two hundred American in gold coin."

"I believe I warned you about this man before you left here. I asked you why didn't he send his own men. No, I wondered why such a powerful man did not ride at the head of the column."

"First, I think he is a coward," Slocum said, refilling their glasses. "Then I figure he thought that no one could rescue her alive. If a gringo got her killed when he tried to get her out of their camp, it would be his fault, not her family's, for going after her."

He slapped the cork back in the bottle and resumed his seat. "The man has no morals. He'll ship her off to some convent, I think, until she agrees to marry someone he considers up to her station."

"Did she say so?"

"No, but she made me promise to get her out if he put her in one."

Goldfarb sat back and nodded, compressing his triple chins. "What do you do next?"

"Listen for word of his plans and help you stave off a slaughter of the Apaches."

"What is that?"

"McVain is in the Madres with his army of renegades. He wasn't a day behind me. He is going to play around up there until you ring the bells down here. Then he will lie in wait for the Apaches to come in."

"A very slick man to slip into the Madres and not one of my people know a thing about it. I think I will have a council meeting. Someone has covered up for him to get by here undetected and into the mountains by this route."

"He had guards stationed at the Devil's Crossing. That was why it took me a week longer to get her home. I had to ride north and take an eagle's route off them."

"Which side are the guards on?"

"This side."

Ruby came up the stairs, and the concern on her face

forced both men to turn for her words.

"A Captain Hernandez is downstairs and has a company of soldiers out in front," she said quietly.

"What did you tell him?" Goldfarb asked her.

"Nothing, that it was siesta time but I would wake you."

"Good. Earlier did the boy take Slocum's horse to the stables?"

"Yes."

"Did Hernandez ask about our guest?"

"No." She shrugged her shoulders and her rounded cleavage quaked.

"Stay here, my friend," Goldfarb said, and rose from the wicker chair. "I will entertain this captain. Chances are he does not even know that you are here or in the area."

"If I am any problem to you—"

"Stay here. I can handle this matter swiftly."

Slocum thanked his friend and slumped down in his own seat to consider his nearly full glass of rye. He heard Goldfarb's greeting to Hernandez from the stairs. What did the officer want? Probably nothing to do with him. He sipped on the smooth liquor and wondered about Estrallia and what she'd been doing since he had left her.

He walked to the French doors and gazed across the green courtyard toward the lofty Madres, almost obscure in the blue haze that clung to the sides. Where were Crook, Al Siebling, and Tom Horn? They should be mounted and in Mexico by this time. Borders wouldn't stop General George Crook; he had little fear of the Mexican forces or their laws.

"They are finally leaving," Ruby whispered.

Half asleep from dozing, Slocum sat upright and thanked her. It had been over an hour since Goldfarb had gone downstairs to meet with the officer. When Slocum paused to listen, he could hear the commands of the soldiers in the street out in front as they shuffled to mount up.

"Guess I dozed off," he said as she gathered their dirty dishes.

"I will let my husband tell you, but this man Hernandez is like a wolf when he looks at you. He gave me cold chills on my arm."

"Sounds like a real nice guy."

"He isn't," she said with a head shake, and left him.

Goldfarb joined him and crossed the room to the doorway. The afternoon wind pressed the silk garment against his great bulk.

"This man Hernandez is joining McVain for the slaughter they plan," he finally said.

"Did he tell you so?"

"No, he didn't need to. The Mexican army never takes a single company of men and rides into the Madres. An entire army, yes. A company, no."

"So you have it figured out that he plans to meet McVain and they will ambush the Apaches. That way the army can say they killed the Apaches and get some recognition." He looked at him for a response.

"That is how close we think alike, Slocum. Yes, I know that is Hernandez's plan."

"So what happens if the Apaches don't come into town to trade."

"It would be best for them. I fear this town's commerce with them is over. Too risky."

"Did he mention looking for me?" Slocum asked.

"No, but he said the American army is in Mexico."

"I figured that." Slocum drew out a quirlie and lighted it. "He say where they are? I'd like to see Horn and Siebling again."

"No, but he bragged that his men would capture the Apaches before the Americans."

Slocum absorbed the man's words as he deeply inhaled the sharp smoke. Slowly he blew a small stream from his pursed lips as he considered everything they knew so far. "I figure that McVain failed to ambush Tomatoes' camp or he'd been out bragging about it already."

"You're right. But tonight I am calling a council meeting

and I intend to find out what traitor let McVain slip into the Madres past us without reporting it. I think we have a spy in our midst and I am going to root him out.''

"Good luck," Slocum said.

13

"She said to tell you, señor, that he has sent her to the Mother of Mary Convent," the small man said with his sombrero clutched in his brown hands.

Slocum considered his options as he silently cursed the jackal who would do such a thing to his own daughter. It was late afternoon, the wind lay still, and dust and wood smoke hung in the air. He had lounged around Paso almost a week waiting for things to develop. No word of Hernandez and McVain's activities in the Madres, nor of the Apaches. This news was not what he hoped for, but he had expected it.

"Tell Estrallia she has my thanks," he said, and paid the man for his long ride.

"What now, my friend?" Goldfarb asked.

"I ride to this convent and get her out."

"But convents are sacred places besides being fortresses. They will hide her in a place you could never find her."

"I found her in an Apache camp. I'll find her in this place."

"Does Don Sallisar know this is your plan?"

Slocum frowned at his host. "I don't think so, unless she told him something in a fit of rage. Why?"

Goldfarb shrugged. "This very well may be a trap."

95

"I'll keep that in mind. I better get Buck ready to travel."

"I hate to see you leave. You make good company."

"I'll be back soon as I get her out of there." That was what he intended anyway.

"Spend the night, it is late. Besides you need to dress more like a *vaquero*. We will dress you more like one so no one will be so suspicious."

"That's a good idea," Slocum agreed as he considered the offer to stay, and finally decided, "I need to reset Buck's shoes, so you have to put up with me another day."

"Wonderful," Goldfarb said, and announced to Ruby that he was staying. She smiled pleased, and went for more liquor for them.

No need to rush off half cocked. It *could* be a trap. Slocum settled in the chair, the glass of rye in his hand. His stiff back could use a good night's sleep in a bed.

At dawn, in the new set of simple clothing Goldfarb had chosen for him, the clothing of a workingman, he tackled the job of resetting the buckskin's shoes. He used the tools in the stable while Goldfarb's *segundo*, Sanchez, squatted close by and observed.

"I could start the forge, señor?" the gray-mustached man offered.

"No, Sanchez," Slocum said between licks with the shoeing hammer on the plate atop the anvil. "This will do this time." He held the shoe up to examine it for flatness; satisfied, he bent over and gathered Buck's right hoof.

Finally, as the heat of the day began to rise, he straightened up, his job completed. "Glad that's done."

"Have a good journey," Sanchez said, and straightened to his feet.

"Thanks, I hope I do," he said, still vexed about how he would get her out of this convent. But he would honor his promise.

Mid-morning, as he prepared to finally leave, Ruby rushed out with a cotton poke full of food. She refused his offer to pay her. At the same time, Goldfarb warned him to be very careful. Everyone looked up at the approach of riders coming off the mountain trail.

"Something is wrong," Goldfarb said with a frown.

"Those are Apaches coming and they have a body wrapped in canvas over a horse." His hand on his gun butt, Slocum blinked in disbelief at the white man who rode in their midst. "That's Tom Horn!"

"What's going on, you old devil?" Tom shouted, kicking his right leg over the saddlehorn to dismount in a jump and come running forward. They hugged and clapped each other on the back.

"Man, you are a sight for sore eyes. I damn sure never expected to see you down here," Tom said. "And that Mexican gitup, I had to blink twice to be certain it was you."

It was the same freckled-faced, grinning Tom, his wheat straw hair and suntan deep as leather; his eye sparkled as they considered each other with out a word.

"Whose body?" Slocum motioned toward the horse.

"That's the bad part," Tom said with a rueful head shake. "That's Captain Crawford."

"Captain Crawford?" Slocum could hardly believe Tom's words. "How did it happen?"

"These scouts, the captain, and myself were slipping up on this camp of renegades and this damn bunch of Mexican irregulars thought we were the enemy and opened fire on us."

"Irregulars?"

"Yeah, there was a Captain Hernandez with them and a bunch of volunteers that he said were part of his outfit. They opened fire on us. Before we could get the shooting stopped between us, they'd killed Captain Crawford. Man, I sure hated it."

"He was a good man."

"The very best," Tom said, and whipped off his hat to scratch the top of his thin blond hair. "He understood more about 'Paches than any man alive. Best one of them that I ever scouted with too."

"Did you see a big man in Scottish dress with them irregulars?"

"No, but there was some soldiers and bunch of border riffraff that this Hernandez called irregulars. He said he had hired them to help him capture the Apaches."

"Scalpers."

"Jesus, you mean the captain was killed by damn scalpers?" Horn threw his weatherbeaten Stetson on the ground in disgust.

"Yes, that's all they are and they work for McVain. Hernandez went up there and joined them a week ago or so."

"When I tell Al and some of them veterans soldiers who rode with Crawford that scalpers killed him, they're liable to storm down here on their own and clean house."

"Be sure they know who it was killed him, not these innocent village people."

"I damn sure will. Say, why don't you come join us? Except for the captain getting his self killed, we're having a gay old time climbing up and down mountains back there chasing the last of the 'Paches."

"I may do that after I finish a little business."

"Good, we could damn sure use you. Say, I'll tell Lieutenant Gatewood and the others that you're planning to come help us. I need to get to a telegraph pronto and wire Arizona about the captain being killed."

"I understand. Be careful. Tell Gatewood I'm looking forward to seeing him again," Slocum said, and shook Horn's hand.

Tom leaped on his horse and waved for the red-bandanna-headband-wearing scouts to ride after him. One of his redskin troopers carried the company guidon flag, made of red and white stripes with a D on it. Head high and with a very proper military seat on his horse, dressed in his half-army, half-Indian clothing, he rode at the head of the column in sharp contrast to the others, who slumped in their saddles in anything but military fashion.

"A friend of yours?" Goldfarb asked from the stairs of the store.

"Yes, Tom Horn. He's lived with the Apaches. Been

married to one. She got killed by a horse falling on her. He speaks the language. A devil-may-care sort of fellow, though.''

''Are you still leaving?'' Goldfarb asked, looking pained over his departure.

''Yes, I promised Lucia I would get her out if her father put her in a convent. One odd thing. Horn just now told me McVain wasn't in sight when Hernandez's soldiers and those scalpers attacked them and shot Captain Crawford.''

''What do you make of that?''

''For some reason, he's slipped out of the Madres.'' Slocum wished he knew why too.

Goldfarb squinted against the noonday sun. ''He's up to no good, that you can count on. I still don't know the traitor in this village. Say, why not wait until morning. It is too late to leave today.''

''Thanks, but I better ride.'' Slocum waved good-bye to Sanchez, Ruby, and Goldfarb, then stood up in the stirrups to trot Buck.

After three days ride, he drew close to the town of Oso and the convent. His clothing from Goldfarb's store made for more typical Mexican dress. He wore blousy white cotton pants, a pull-over cotton shirt, and a multicolored vest of thick rolled cotton. The high-crown sombrero was held by a leather throat latch under his chin. He hoped he appeared less of a gringo in his costume.

He bought food in the village from a street vendor for an excuse to look around. She was an ample-bodied woman who talked freely with him about the weather, his yellow horse that she admired and how lucky a poor workingman had been able to buy such a beast.

''He belongs to my patron,'' Slocum said as he chewed the dry stringy meat and beans in her tortilla.

''Ah, do you belong with the six men who came with the black coach a few days ago? They were *pistoleros* too.''

''What valuable cargo did they bring?''

''A daughter of a rich patron was taken to the convent.''

"Did you see her?"

"No, the shades were drawn, but gossip says she is very pretty." The woman looked around to be sure no one was in earshot. Then she hissed, "They say she is pregnant with a black man's child."

"Oh, what a shame. I would take one more please," Slocum said, and dug in his pocket for a ten-centavo piece. "Why did they take her to this place?"

The woman's brown eyes darted from side to side to be certain no one on the street was close enough to hear her. "To save a scandal?"

"A scandal, huh?"

"A half-black child, would that not be shame enough?" She busied herself laddling the steaming contents into the V-shaped tortilla.

"Why not a wedding?"

The woman shook her head as she handed him the white flour wrapped dish "Never. He would be below her class. Besides they would not want such a child as an heir." Then she smiled at him. "I would take it and raise it with my children."

"And your husband, would he take it in as his own?"

"Oh, señor, my poor Jacquin is dead. He was killed by bandits last year."

"I'm sorry," Slocum said.

He finished his meal, then gave the woman two pesos *for the little ones*. She nearly cried at his generosity, and waved good-bye to him as he mounted Buck.

"—and God be with you, hombre," she cried after him.

Slocum touched his hat in salute and rode off. He certainly needed someone with him on this mission. Outside the village he selected a place to stay for the rest of the day. In the shade of some stunted cottonwoods beside a small stream, he napped. Buck grazed in the bottoms; a small herd of curious goats scolded both of them. After sundown, Slocum intended to storm the convent that stood like a fortress on the hill overlooking the *jacaels* and huts. He did not want any undue curiosity about his presence, so he decided to lay low.

• • •

Darkness had settled on the land. Dull pearl starlight glowed on the plastered buildings, and an occasional cur dog barked at something. In the distance Slocum could hear a guitar and someone singing about a caballero. The raucous unmistakable laughter of a *puta* in a cantina came above Buck's soft hoof-fall as Slocum rode up the dirt street toward the shiplike dark bulk of the convent on the hill.

He dismounted nearby and hitched Buck to a mesquite tree. Above him the arches of the bell tower shone against the star-filled sky. There was no moon now and there would only be a sliver later—a perfect night to prowl. He quickly ascended the stairs, curious about how the great doors, shrouded in deep shadows, could be opened.

Then as if out of nowhere the muzzle of a gun jabbed him in the back and a coarse voice followed. "Put your hands in the air, gringo!"

14

"A damn trap," escaped Slocum's lips as his hands flew skyward and the man pulled the Colt from his holster. He closed his eyes to shut out his despair. A knot grew in his belly as he silently cursed his own stupidity; someone had planned it well and the jaws of the steel had snapped him in them.

"So, hombre, at last we meet." The figure wore a uniform in the darkness; shorter than Slocum, he smelled of cigars and rum.

"Oh, I think we've met before," Slocum said, wondering who else was with the man. He could make out the hard-billed cap of a *federale* officer. Several more soles shuffled around sounding gritty on the stairs of the convent.

"Where was that?" the officer demanded.

"When I was turning cow pies over looking for dung beetles."

One of the soldiers drove his gun's barrel hard into Slocum's back. "You won't be laughing in the jail, hombre."

"Who's laughing? Who the hell are you?" Slocum asked over his shoulder, realizing he was surrounded by a half-dozen soldiers, besides the officer.

"I am Captain Pino of the *federales*. Here, Sergeant Ortega, you guard this hombre with your life. If he escapes it will be your neck."

"*Sí*, captain."

"Where is the ring that you stole?" Pino asked in Slocum's face.

"What ring?"

Pino drove a hard fist into Slocum's gut. "If you return the ring, the judge may cut your sentence."

"What ring?" Slocum managed, though his breath came short. The pain in his belly was sharp enough to hurt.

"I am certain that the Sergeant Ortega here can loosen your lips on the whereabouts of the jewelry that you stole from Don Sallisar. I will be at the cantina if you have any problems, Sergeant."

"Damn nice meeting you, Pino. By the way who told you I was coming?" Slocum shouted after the officer as rough hands on both sides took his arms and forced him to walk down the road.

"The man you stole the ring from, Don Sallisar, said that you would try to kidnap his daughter again."

"Never did it in the first place!" Slocum shouted, but the hard blow of a rifle butt to his shoulder sent him staggering forward and silenced him.

"I don't have his damn ring!" Slocum slurred for the five hundredth time. His vision was blurred by his blackened eyes, and his face ached from the repeated blows. How long would their interrogation go on? For days, he supposed, until they wore out or he confessed. His protests about being an American citizen only drew more blows from his accusers.

Finally rough hands lifted him from the chair that he had been bound to, and they dragged his battered form to the cell where they unceremoniously dumped him belly-down on a cot. The iron door clanged shut and the unmistakable key sound clicked the bolt in place. Totally exhausted, he closed his eyes to the pain in his body as the half-dozen soldiers outside his cell cussed his resolve and promised him worse treatment in the future.

"Kiss my ass," he mumbled into the sour-smelling blan-

ket under his face. For the time being he had worn them
out with no satisfaction. Unless he escaped, though, they
would be fresh the next day to resume their torture. No
way, could he even imagine getting out of the thick-walled
jail, he closed his eyes and slept.

"This man is guilty, Your Honor!" the small man in the
business suit shouted to the judge.

Slocum had lost track of days and nights. He knew as
he stood before the high bench, the fiery little prosecutor
next to him was determined to have him sentenced to a
long prison term. Pain filled his body and mind, and Slocum could not make his thoughts connect. The hurting in
every muscle had settled in as a dullness that made anything
he had to do mentally a great task.

"What do you have to say for yourself?" the stern-faced
man in the black robes demanded.

"I never took any ring. Would you ask the Don's wife
if this is true?"

"Your Honor, there is no need to ask the Donna anything. Her husband Don Sallisar had testified under oath
this man, under the guise of a rich American businessman,
came to their hacienda and then stole a ruby gold ring from
the Donna's collection. Why would she say anything different from her husband?"

"Good point, Prosecutor." The judge turned his stern
gaze back to Slocum. "Captain Pino told me you also
planned to desecrate a convent?"

"Damned if I know that word." Slocum frowned as he
listened for the answer.

The judge rapped the gavel. "Señor No Name, who they
call Slocum, I sentence you to ten years at hard labor for
your crime of stealing the ring from Don Sallisar and five
years for threatening a place of religion."

"Your Honor, could you make it five more?" Slocum
asked in disgust.

The judge frowned.

"It's for what I intend to do next to this pus-gutted sergeant who has beaten on me for the past three weeks.''

The judge frowned as he looked down at him. ''What is that?''

Slocum whirled and despite the leg irons drove his knee into Ortega's crotch, and the man doubled over in pain. Then with a downstroke, Slocum drove the handcuffs into the back of the noncom's head sending him face down to the floor. Then the lights went out, and Slocum didn't wake up until he found himself lying in the bed of an ox cart that creaked over the bumpy roadway.

He could see through his swollen eyes the green uniforms of the *federales* on horseback close by. The rest of his body felt as if it would break in two any moment.

Vaguely he recalled the judge's sentence—fifteen years rotting in a Mexico jail. He could hardly conceive surviving such a sentence. But there was nothing he could do about it for the moment. He drew a deep breath up his swollen nose; the vile odor of feces and sweat from his body was enough to make him puke if there had been a thing in his empty stomach. The wagon lurched on every rock and jarred his sanity.

The prison warden was a hawk-nosed man who sat behind a great polished wooden desk and beat his palm with a riding quirt. From the sound it made when he slapped it into his hand, Slocum knew it was weighted with lead.

''So the *mucho* tough gringo is here at last.''

''Say, 'yes, sir,' '' the guard on his right said sharply in Slocum's ear.

''Yes, sir.''

''Ah, Tomas, this one needs to learn a few lessons, no?'' the warden asked the man who had spoken in Slocum's ear.

''Yes, I think so.''

''Lock him in the hold for a while. He looks close to breaking.''

''Yes, sir.''

''Slocum, you will learn that to conform to our rules is

how you will survive in here."

"Yes, sir," he said, but his thoughts were on the yellow light flooding in the window and his freedom. Then he was roughly dragged away and locked up in the belly of the prison.

Days and nights in the lightless hole seemed as one. Every two days they exchanged his slop bucket. An old prisoner came shuffling in wearing leg irons and carried it off while the guards held Slocum at bay with a great dog, an Airedale that acted ferociously on the heavy chain that one of the guards gripped with both his hands. Slocum hoped it never slipped. The other held a candle lamp and a pistol in the opposite hand. They were armed for bear, and it was his only diversion, coming every other day.

Meager food arrived twice a day; a hiss, and then a bowl was handed in the small opening in the door. The rest of the time, he was by himself in the bowels of the prison, alone without voices or even sounds. The crickets played a symphony. He lay on the iron bench and listened to them for hours. His leg irons had grown loose as his legs shrank away from them, and now they severely chafed his ankles.

With no way to escape, he became filled with a new-found resolve. He began regimented exercises to help his body drive out the stiffness. Various calisthenics and running in place for a mile—he counted each step as three feet, and he had to do 1760 strides to reach his goal. He did them after every meal. It helped occupy his time, and his body soon began to heal from the blows and bruises of his captors.

His jailers would sooner or later grow tired of his solitary confinement. Once in the prison population, he could then calculate escaping. His physical condition would serve him well if the opportunity to escape ever presented itself.

He was awaken by voices in the hallway. A familiar voice carried as the cell door was unlocked and shoved open. The flood of two lanterns was more than his eyes could stand; though his lids were slitted, he recognized the familiar plaid kilts and the great girth of McVain in the doorway.

"By gawd, you went and did it, huh, Slocum?"

He rose, realizing he was dressed in filthy rags that hung on his skeleton form. "Took you long enough to get here."

McVain wrinkled his great nose at the stench. "I guess you'll be wanting out of this pisser?"

"Lead the way."

McVain's laughter shattered the tomb's closeness. "Aye, they haven't beat all the fire from you, have they? Come along, laddie, we've got a hundred prime scalps to collect."

Slocum shrugged and then looked around and in the blaze of lights. For the first time he could see the entire small cell carved out of rock.

"Good-bye, old world, may I never see the likes of you ever again," he muttered to himself, and then he glared hard in the face of the guard holding up the light and waiting for him. Defensively, the man drew himself back to the wall to escape Slocum's wraith. Instead Slocum shook his head in disgust, and set out after the other lamp ahead up the tunnel. He followed the boisterous sound of McVain's voice talking to the other guard.

Outside in the prison yard, his eyes ached in the brilliant sunlight. But he gulped in the hot air and for the first time in God knows how long, he experienced a new sense—a notion he would soon be free. The thought exhilarated him as he sloughed along in the leg irons. Freedom wasn't far away, and the big Scotsman in his red plaid outfit was going to be his way out.

"Give them a bath and get their new clothing," McVain told the guard in charge.

Five men, including Slocum, stood in line, all gringos. Word was out that there were no Mexican prisoners that hated prison bad enough to go fight the dreaded Apaches to get out.

Step one was the removal of their leg irons. Slocum wanted to lift his legs to the ceiling once he was rid of the confining chains.

"My name's Red Meyers," the big man next to him in line said as they waited for the blacksmith to free the last ones.

"Slocum's mine. You ready to go hunt down Apaches?" He repeatedly lifted his knees, not quite certain he was really free of the irons.

"I would fight alligators bare-handed to get out of this place. How about you?"

Slocum shrugged. "They couldn't be much worse."

"You been in the hole ain't you?"

"Yeah, You can tell?"

"Your eyes. I didn't figure you was crying over your good luck."

"Not yet."

"Yeah, what's this talk about a bath?" Meyers asked with a concerned frown of disapproval. "It might give a man 'nuemonia.'"

"If they want us clean to get out of here, hell, I'll take the chance," Slocum said.

Both men laughed. There was a Johnny Yeager—a boy of perhaps eighteen, a German called Sleigal, and a cross-eyed man who called himself the Grande Kid. Slocum, Yeager, Meyers, Sleigal, and Grande all filed into the bathroom under the hard gazes of two armed guards. The smell of soap and hot water wafted up Slocum's nose like a dream too good to be true as he considered the tin tubs filled with hot water lined up for them.

Once up to his neck in the facility, he closed his eyes and savored the pleasure the near-boiling water brought to his filthy body. Mechanically, he began to lather himself in every place that he could reach. The sharp ash odor of the lye soap cut deep in the nostrils, but he grinned away the discomfort and continued in his quest to get clean.

Finally dressed in prison-made clothing, all five saw McVain and one of his men standing out in the yard waiting for them.

"You guys ain't exactly angels," McVain said to them. "I'm handcuffing you. And anyone makes a break for it, he gets shot for desertion. Am I clear?"

"What if we get into a shootout with Apaches going to your place?" the Kid asked.

"Then I'll cut you loose. Savvy?"

"I guess, just asking."

"Any more questions," McVain asked; when none came, he then motioned for his man to cuff them.

Slocum could see the warden standing on the second-story balcony. The man was slapping his palm with the loaded quirt.

"Good-bye, you old sumbitch," Slocum muttered to himself. Cuffed with his hands in front of him, Slocum fell in line behind the redhead. They were headed for the gate, and despite his hands being bound, he felt relieved as the hard caliche ground of the prison yard met the stiff soles of his ill-fitting new shoes—for the last time, he hoped. No telling how long he had been there—a month or two, no doubt—but he was getting out anyhow some fourteen years early.

The line of hipshot ponies looked inviting at the rail beside the huge towering wall. Another McVain man sat on horseback cradling a Winchester just in case anyone got foolish enough to break and run. Slocum ignored him.

"Set your stirrups to suit yourself," McVain ordered once they'd randomly chosen their mounts.

Slocum's fingers fumbled with excitement as he reset the latigo leathers. How had it all happened so quickly? How did McVain know he was inside the prison and pick him out? He had heard for years that was where the man's recruits came from, but still, the coincidence seemed too great as he mounted up.

In the saddle with the short-coupled horse between his knees, he drew a deep breath as he searched the mesquite-clad dry flats that surrounded the prison and studied the sawtooth purple mountains in the distance. Free was a wonderful four-letter word. He breathed in the creosote-perfumed air and felt chaffed already by the stiff new clothing.

"Glad you could join me," McVain said, riding his big horse in close.

"Yeah, I always wanted to work for someone like you. To see how you operated, anyway."

"You'll see soon enough. Glad your curiosity is up, though,'cause I thought the same damn thing about you, laddie. Let's ride." He raised a hand in the air and waved for all to follow him on his galloping horse.

15

"There ain't very damn much going on here," Meyers said under his breath, showing his disgust at his handcuffed hands to Slocum. Above them towered the thick pine-forested slopes of the Madres. McVain's camp was located high enough up in the cool mountain air that it felt rewarding after the prison's heat and the breathless atmosphere of the desert.

"They're waiting for word from their scouts to come in and tell them where the Apaches are located," Slocum said softly enough for only the big man to hear.

"You use to scout for the U.S. Army, someone said."

"A long time ago."

"What about it? Can this bunch of cutthroats and rapers here fight them Apaches?"

"If McVain's got enough good guns and plenty of ammunition he can. But in the past he's been mostly attacking their camps, killing squaws and kids."

"Guess anyone could kill them. There's about a dozen or so of his regular men and the five of us. How many Apaches bucks are in this bunch."

"Not many more. Why?"

"Whew, I thought we was pulling some kinda Custer shit up here, going up against a thousand of them red sumbitches."

"Hell, there ain't never been that many Chiricahuas if they all were down here. Maybe a hundred or hundred and fifty in total, counting women and children, and those are in a half-dozen bands to my count."

"Why are they so set on capturing such a pitiful few damn Injuns?"

"Because they're Apaches and a half-dozen can lay down more destruction than an army as well as outmaneuver an army at the same time."

Meyers made a distasteful scowl with his mouth. "Why don't he uncuff us?"

Slocum shrugged; he had no answer. Obviously McVain was not convinced he could fully trust his latest recruits. Slocum knew more about his fellow parolees than he had the first day. Drunk and mad, Meyers had caved four men's heads in with an ax handle before they subdued him in a cantina fight. The young-looking boy had been in prison for using a Bowie knife on a whore he got mad at. She supposedly had laughed at his best effort at an erection. He had opened her up from the crotch to her throat.

The Grande Kid was in for buggering two little boys. They caught him doing it in an alley, and the women that witnessed his act tried to beat him to death with sticks and clubs. The Kid claimed it was a lie, that the real reason for him being in prison was he'd killed a couple of *federales* and some rich guy in a shootout over a beautiful woman.

The German made it to jail by printing counterfeit money, a fact that intrigued the Kid no end. He followed the poor man about inquiring how hard it was to print real-looking money.

"It is gawdamn hard to print the real-looking money," Sleigal finally said aloud to silence his questioner. "I got caught doing it and now I'm in this wild place with cut-throats and killers and molesters of small boys waiting for the damn Apaches to kill me."

"I never touched no damn boys!"

"Funny damn thing, everyone in the gawdamn prison said you did."

"Lies, lies! All of it was damn lies by the family of them men I shot."

"Only ones that I think got shot was them little boys."

"Listen, you damn kraut-eating sumbitch, I get out of these cuffs and get a damn gun, I'll blow your ass to kingdom come."

"Yeah, well, maybe them Apaches will corn-hole you first," Sleigel threw his head back and laughed aloud at the shorter red-faced man before him. "Then you will know how them little boys felt, huh?"

Muttering to himself, the Kid left the campfire area and wandered off toward the shallow river. The German shook his head after the man, then took a seat on the ground with the other parolees. Slocum looked up; there was a horse coming, maybe one of McVain's scouts returning with news. At last maybe they'd have some action and a better chance for him to escape. He watched the blue green junipers for the rider to emerge. It was an Indian and Slocum looked away; he tried to act disinterested, for some of McVain's regulars were always scrutinizing them for some kind of telltale sign. He didn't want to appear too anxious about anything.

After a short while, McVain came outside his wall tent and looked across at the parolees. "Get up here, you gawdamn convicts, and get those irons off. We're going Injun hunting. Just remember, laddies, you make one wrong move and you're dead. You understand?"

A man called Quel undid the handcuffs. McVain issued each man a Colt in a holster with twenty or so rounds under the loops. He shoved the wrapped gun and rig into Slocum's gut. Neither man looked down at the gun exchange; both locked stares with each other.

"You try something, gunfighter, and your ass is dead," McVain said through his teeth.

"Who's trying something," Slocum said, slow and deliberate. "I came to see your boys in action."

"Make you damn rich man, Slocum, if you help me."

"I can stand to be rich. I never been that in my whole life."

"You follow orders and you'll do just that."

"Good," Slocum said, and headed for his horse, rolling out the belt and strapping it around his waist.

"Slocum!" He whirled at the words.

"You remember me? Garnett's my name. I'm the one you pistol-whipped in town that day." The dark-faced man in the derby hat stepped off his horse, his hand ready to go for his gun.

"Nice to meet you," Slocum said, giving him a casual glance and turning his back.

"Come back here! You yellow-belly sumbitch, I aim to outdraw you."

Slocum shook his head and walked on as if he'd dismissed the man's threat. The titter of laughter from the others would not help, Slocum knew as the man reached out and grabbed his shoulder to twist him around.

Slocum's haymaker came from his knees, drove the wind out of the man's solar plexus, and bent him forward. Slocum's next fist sent the man's head flying back, and he landed on his back without moving. His six-gun spilled out of his holster. Slocum's boot toe sent it spinning across the ground.

"Garnett ain't the smartest man in this outfit," McVain said with a rueful shake of his head from where he had observed the fracas. "Everyone of you be ready to ride in thirty minutes."

Slocum settled on the ground with the other parolees out of habit and drew out the .44-caliber Colt. He opened the side gate and rolled the cylinder on the back of his forearm to inspect the chambers.

"Your gun's empty," Meyers said with a deep inhale of shock. "Did you know that?"

"Nope, but I do now," Slocum said, his gaze set on McVain's tent and the closed flap. Trap or was it unplanned? He would know in a few days, if he lived that long. How in the hell would he ever shake McVain? There had to be a way. With no cuffs and a gun, he at least stood a chance of doing it. Better go saddle the crow bait. He didn't intend to be left behind.

• • •

McVain sent his scouts ahead of the column. Single file, they climbed the steep face of the mountain through the tall timber. Slocum noted all their mounts were grass-soft and soon were sweating and puffing. He wished for the buckskin, and wondered what peon had him pulling a wooden plow or cart. Maybe the fat sergeant possessed him, or even Captain Peno had him. He could sure use his stamina in the event that an escape opportunity came to light. At this point, he could have turned Buck downhill and they'd have never caught him going off the sheer mountain face. If he turned the stumbling pony under him, he would certainly end up at the base in a ball, both of them dead.

They rode over several more ranges of mountains. Finally McVain called a halt, but almost too late for the ponies they rode. Slocum's mount was so spent it hung its head and snorted wearily in desperation. He dismounted and loosened the cinch.

"You've about killed the horseflesh," he said to McVain as he rode by. "What's next."

"Their camp's right over the hill," McVain said with a pleased grin behind his full beard, and pushed his horse on.

Whose camp? Were they just women and children? McVain never was known for fighting men.

"He say them Apaches were close?" Meyers asked under his breath.

Slocum nodded. They were very close if his scouts knew anything. Whose camp? Natise's? Geronimo's? Tomatoes's? Or another's. Be interesting to know. And the girl Lucia—perhaps Estrallia would know where they held her. He should worry more about his own safety and escaping. One thing for certain, he damn sure couldn't do anything on the jaded bay.

That might be McVain's overall plan; run the horses into the ground so they had no choice but to stay and fight the Apaches. Not so dumb either, unless they had to ride to save their lives; then it would simply be too bad.

"Spread out along this ridge. The camp is in the canyon. We should get a good place to shoot them from above," McVain told them. "You new men better take your share of shots or you'll for certain be Apache bait. Am I clear?"

"Yes, sir," came their reply.

Slocum felt watched as he moved after Meyers.

"Is it hard to scalp a man?" the man asked over his shoulder.

"I guess it's not as much work as skinning buffalo," Slocum said, still looking for an opportunity. The notion of shooting down defenseless children and squaws was more than he could stand.

They crept through the trees to the edge of sheer rock face. The smell of campfire smoke curled upward out of the canyon, assailed his nostrils, and formed a sinking feeling inside Slocum's stomach. McVain's scouts had found a mountain camp.

He studied the thick tree trunks that clung to hillside beneath his position. Would they offer enough cover for him to make a run downhill to warn the Indians? If he burst into their camp, the Apaches would probably never believe he was trying to help them. Both sides would end up shooting at him.

One of McVain's men came by then, hissing at them to get down on their bellies, watch for the big man's signal, and be ready to start firing.

"Meyers, start shooting when I get past that big tree down there."

"Huh?" The man's eyes widened in disbelief.

"Just do as I say. I ever get able to do something for you, I will."

"You'll be killed." He looked in disbelief at Slocum.

"May save a few innocent women and youngsters," Slocum said under his breath and was already on his feet bent low. He leaped off the five-foot rim bluff and landed on his shoe heels running downhill.

Bullets began to whiz through the pine boughs. Meyers was doing his part. Below he heard the surprised cries of the women as well as McVain's loud screams of displeasure.

"I'll get you Slocum, you sumbitch!' I'll cut out your balls for ruining this!'' His great voice echoed over and over as Slocum skidded and ran down the last hundred yards, cutting back and forth to use the trees for cover.

Out of breath, at the base of the slope, he leaped the small trickle of water and spotted a wide-eyed pony tethered near a grass wickiup. Spooked by the rounds of bullets raining on the camp, the horse jerked away. The shouts of the fleeing women and children running away were enough for Slocum—if you gave an Apache a two-minute head start, then you would probably never see him again.

Slocum jerked up the rope and mounted in one fluid move. Bent low on the animal's back, he sent the pony plunging down out of the canyon beside the small watercourse. Free at last, he reached back and adjusted the Colt; if he could avoid the Apaches and McVain, maybe he could go back to living his own life.

The girl Lucia still needed his help, but where ever was she being held? As the shots of McVain's men grew further away and the pony carried him down the canyon he wondered about her plight. The witch would know, he would ride over and see her.

16

A single fleeing Apache woman with a baby in her arms glanced over her shoulder at him before she quickly disappeared into the brush. The look of fear in her brown eyes hurt him. He whipped the pony on down the canyon, guilty that he could not offer to help her, nor turn aside the enemy coming off the mountain for her. She must find some place to outwait them.

He reached where the canyon throat opened, and turned the hard-breathing pony westward. He allowed it to trot a while, satisfied few of McVains's stock could ever catch up with them. He adjusted his seat on the pony's back. Bareback was not his choice of ways to ride, but he would never complain, not with McVain's efforts to raid the *rancheria* thwarted and himself out of the scalpers' camp.

At nightfall, he drew near the village. The pony had long tired. Grass-fed, he lacked the stamina of a grain-fed animal, and would be of little use once he reached Santa Cristo. In a week or so the animal would recover if Slocum turned him loose, but he would need a fresh one to ride after he spoke to Estrallia.

He rode past the sleepy guard, who only mumbled, "Good evening."

In the square, he left the pony at the hitch rack in front of the noisy cantina. While he licked his cracked lips, he considered the enticing smell of raw liquor mingled with cigar smoke that wafted out from behind the lighted door-way and batwing doors. No time for such things.

Certain no one saw him slip into the shadows, he circled the square until he could rap on her door.

"Who is it?" a sleepy voice asked from inside.

"Señora! My poor wife—"

"Who?" she demanded, opening the door only a crack.

He shouldered it open enough to enter, and covered her protesting mouth with a kiss. "There," he finally said, "that should keep you quiet for the time being."

"How did you escape prison?" she whispered in disbelief.

"They let me out for good behavior."

"Lies, lies. How did you escape?"

"I went bounty-hunting with McVain and I quit him in the process. I thought witches knew everything."

She shook her head in the darkness of the room. "Sometimes we only can guess. But I worry they will come after you here."

"I know, and I can't stay long," he said, drawing her ripe body against his. "But I had to see you."

"Oh, yes, you come so often. You are shameless. But I have worried about you for many days."

Her closeness only fired his need for her more as she toyed with his shirt buttons. "You are dressed so strange," she said.

"Prison clothing."

"Yes, you will need others. In the daylight everyone can tell who was your tailor."

"How can we do it?"

"Take them off your body first," she teased, opening the shirt and then running her hands over his muscle-hard body.

They were both thinking alike, he decided as he lifted her blouse off over her head. Her hard breasts soon poked into his belly as she hugged him. Out of breath with excitement and their nakedness in the darkness that engulfed them, they stood atop a pile of clothes.

He swept her up in his arms and drew a girlish laugh

from her; then she sealed his effort with a hard kiss. He carried her sumptuous form, savoring the honey of her mouth with his tongue, to the small rear bedroom. There he laid her on the narrow cot.

Sprawled on top of her, he gently pushed her legs apart and moved between them. Her soft cry of pleasure at his entry only drove him harder. The ropes under the mattress protested at his effort, and they both became lost in the passion of the night.

A light was on in the next room when he awoke alone in the bed. His eyes searched for his clothing; he turned his ear to listen to the soft titter of women's voices. His clothes were in that room. There were more women than Estrallia in the next room, and he lay on the bed in Adam's uniform. In addition, his bladder was about to burst and he was unsure of the night jar's location. There was nothing else he could do but wrap himself like some Indian in the thin blanket from the bed and step out the back door. It must be close to sunrise, the coolness of the night told him, though he could not see the eastern horizon for any sign. His chore completed, he returned to discover the purpose of the women.

"Good evening," he said, and drew a titter of snickers from the women for Estrallia's benefit. They were sewing, and Estrallia shoved new pants into his hand as she directed him into the back room to change.

They were the leather pants of a *vaquero,* much better than the loose cotton ones that the prison made. He pulled them on and discovered there were no buttons in the fly. He looked up and she stepped in, and he held the closure shut.

"I had to see if they would fit first," she said, pulling them down impatiently.

"Thanks," he said as he finishing removing them for her. "The girl . . ."

"Lucia Sallisar? She is being held at a place called San Maria." She took the pants, her voice near a whisper as she continued. "There are some sisters there and she is receiving instruction. There is nothing you can do for her."

"That will be my judgment. A horse?"

"Elainia Cordova's husband is getting one and a saddle. You do not understand this is not an affair of people, it is an affair of the Church. She wishes to be there." Estrallia frowned at his stubbornness.

"She can tell me that and I will leave her."

"Good, you have not lost all your senses."

"My clothes?"

"They will be ready in a short while. I went and got all my friends from their sleep to come help me. Soon they must go home and cook for their families."

"I understand and I can pay them."

She shook her head, obviously dismayed that he did not understand why they did such a thing—not for money, he decided as she left him.

An hour later, dressed in his *vaquero* clothing and a new Chiluhaua sombrero, he strapped on the .45. For his money his own muzzle-loaded .31-caliber revolvers were better side arms than the newer one, but they were in the hands of Captain Peno or some Mexican official by this time.

"You must remember that you are not God, hombre, and if the girl wants to be there you must not take her away."

"I savvy all that," he said, holding her lightly in his arms and looking down into her face. "Any word about the U.S. Army?"

"They say many are soon coming here. Then they go to the mountains."

That was no help. He hated to hide under the army's petticoat, but he might have to until his business was complete in the Madres. Both Siebling and Tom Horn had invited him back. He bet Crook was furious that Crawford had been killed. Captain Crawford had understood the Apaches better than most men living.

Perhaps if Slocum had stayed with the scalpers he'd have learned how deliberate the captain's death had been. Someone might have opened up and spilled the beans while they were drunk or something. If he thought for one minute that McVain had plotted the man's death, he would go back and even the score for the captain.

"You aren't even listening," she said, jarring him to awareness. "The horse is in the alley. You can ride out the small gate that they wheel out the horse-droppings through."

"Trouble at the front one?" he asked with a head toss in the direction of the gate.

"Yes, the sergeant is out there and he is parading around like the new president of Mexico."

"I don't fear him."

"I know, but he has no idea you are here. This way he can tell no one either."

"What about the pony I rode in on?"

"He never saw it. Ramon put it out to pasture before the sergeant awoke this morning. Quit worrying."

"I will. But I don't know when I'll be back to see you," he said, taking her shoulders in his hands.

"Don't be so long coming back." Then she drove a doubled fist into his rock-hard belly. Then, chewing her lower lip, she waved her still-tight fist in his face.

He drew her close and hugged her. "I could never have done this without you."

"I know," she said. "I know."

Slocum skirted the main road south en route to San Maria. He knew the village where he headed was small, but he needed to learn about it en route. The young roan horse, while thin and untrained, made a stout satisfactory mount. He reined better after two days of riding him. Each day, along the route, Slocum had taken his meals with small rancheros and their families, always paying a small sum for their generosity.

A man who pays, he knew, is never denied shelter or food again. Nor is such a man often betrayed to the inquisitive *federales*. There was no love between the small Mexican rancher and the soldiers—hungry, the military would eat his cattle without compensation.

By the shadow of a quarter moon he rode into the small village. A desert village, San Maria never had been threatened by the Apaches, so there were no fortress walls to secure the *jacals* and casas inside. The church property stood on a small rise, and the bell tower loomed out at night against the starlight horizon. Slocum had no intention of riding up to the door. He feared a new trap, so he dismounted before the local cantina, racked the horse, and went inside.

"*Mia* amigo," the bartender said to welcome him with open arms when he entered.

"*Gracias*," Slocum said to the man, and ordered a bottle of whiskey. He drew out a quirlie and struck a lucifer under the bar's rolled edge. Slowly he drew off it and studied the men in the place. Most looked like simple men anxious to forget the day's heat and their labor. He saw no cold-fish eyes of gunfighters and men for hire.

"You are a stranger," the barkeep said.

"Yes, I have been working in Chilhuahua."

"A *vaquero* by your clothes?" The man gave a head toss to indicate his dress.

"Yes, my wife made them," Slocum said, to sound like a simple man who punched cattle.

"She is a very skilled woman. Why are you here?"

"I am out of work. The Apaches burned down the rancho where I worked. The patron has given up on it."

"*Sí*, I understand your plight. There is much damage the red devils have done. But there is no work here either." He shook his head warily.

"Fine. I will ride on."

"Once I could say there were many ranches needing a good man like yourself. Today . . ." He threw his hands up in surrender. "Today nothing."

Slocum sampled the bottle in his glass. It was not the best, but the best in the man's stock. He sipped the whiskey and listened to a customer sing about the Wild Caballero while his friend strummed the guitar.

It was a folk song of the land. The singer raised his voice for the chorus and others toasted him with their drinks.

Slocum did too. He was like the wild caballero running free across this land with his freedom endangered by the men who sought him.

He and the bartender spoke of the lack of rain, the poor prices for cattle. Even the Americans did not come to buy as they did before. Was he an American?

"My father—" Slocum never finished before the man asked, "Mormon?"

"*Sí.*"

The bartender nodded emphatically that he knew about such polygamist offspring who were members of the society too.

"There is a famous mission here?" Slocum asked the man.

He shook his head no and dismissed the notion.

"Oh, but I heard there was a shrine here. A special place?" Slocum acted like a man disappointed with his discovery.

"A few sisters who teach is all, and a priest who was away for a meeting with the bishop."

"There is nothing or no one up there like a politician seeking absolution?"

"Maybe a month ago. A don's daughter was sent there. But no one has ever seen her except the women who help clean."

"What was she there for?" he asked.

"Because her father did not approve of her suitors. Maybe that too is a rumor. Maybe she wished to become a nun. Who knows of such things. My wife goes there and prays and prays."

"You don't go often?"

"At Easter, maybe." The bartender shrugged and then drew two beers for his singing customers.

"Did she have guards when she came?"

"Yes, but they went back in a few days. Who would bother her in such a holy place?"

"I don't know."

"No one," he said with finality as he ducked out from behind the bar and took the beers to the balladeers.

Slocum sipped his whiskey and let the liquor mellow his thoughts. A woman who cleaned would know where in the church she was kept, if she was a prisoner.

At dawn he squatted on his boot heels and waited on the main street that led to the church. The two women wore *reboosas* over their heads as they headed for Mass. He watched them approach, wondering if they were workers or worshippers.

"Buenas días!" he said, rising and removing his hat at their approach. "Excuse my rudeness, but are you going to pray?"

"*Sí?*" Both were older women, and looked with interest at each other, then at him for what this stranger wanted of them.

"Do you know Lucia Sallisar?"

They looked at each other and frowned. For a minute he wondered if they even knew of her existence inside.

"The girl from the hacienda?" one woman said.

"*Sí*. Is she all right?"

Both women grew very rigid.

"Please, I must know, for my mother was her maid and she has cried every day for this girl. She prays and burns many candles that she is all right and she has made me come here on this foolish mission to learn of her happiness." He lowered his head humbly and made the sign of a cross.

The full-faced one looked at her friend for strength, then hesitantly spoke. "She should pray harder for her because they fear this girl is going mad. The sisters must keep her locked in her room. Your mother's fears are not ungrounded."

"If I brought my mother, could she see her? I mean talk at her door or anything?"

"You should ask Sister Mary."

"Yes, ask her," the quieter one agreed.

"Is this room safe?"

"Safe?"

"Does it have locks?"

"Yes. And bars on the outside. It is in the back of the convent where the sisters live."

"What will I tell my poor mother? Lucia has been like a daughter to her."

"I would seek a priest to tell her the news."

"Oh, yes," the second one agreed.

"*Gracias*. You are fine ladies like my own mother. I will think of a way to tell her when I return home."

The women went on their way while he resumed his place at the wall. He recalled Lucia's words—*come and get me out*. Was he too late? With his time in prison and the weeks spent with the scalpers, perhaps a few months had elapsed. Had she gone insane in that length of time? He closed his sun-sore eyes to the notion and let his head pound at the temples. Bad whiskey always made bad hangovers. He knew better.

If he only knew how to get her out so he could go do what he needed to do—needed to do? Deep inside he felt an urge to re-join Horn and Siebling for old time sake. He'd do that right after he got her free.

17

"Lucia!" he hissed as he removed the bar. The lock would be something else, but he had a blacksmith hammer. Why didn't she answer him? And where were the sisters? All asleep, he hoped.

"Lucia." No reply. How bad did she want out of there? Was she drugged or was this another wild-goose chase like the last time when they captured him and sentenced him to jail under those phoney charges.

Both hands grasped the wooden hammer handle, and he struck the lock with the hammer. The hasp fell open in the dim candlelight.

"Slocum, is that you?" came a small voice on the other side of the door.

"You do want out, don't you?" he asked in a loud whisper.

"Yes, but I don't have any clothes to wear except this shift."

"We can buy clothes." No time to worry about what she had on. He shouldered open the thick wood door. She bolted out into his arms and smothered him with wet kisses. Her hard body pressed against him, bringing up all sorts of notions.

"We haven't got any time for this," he said, feeling like a stern father. He checked down the hallway, half-expecting one of the sisters to turn from vapor into a living form armed with a shotgun leveled at them. With her by the hand, he dragged her down the hall, through the main door to the convent he had pried open, and outside to the waiting horses.

She looked around and hugged herself in the thin white gown.

"Mount up, we haven't got time to be modest." He boosted her into the saddle of the spare horse.

"You came," she swooned, seated atop the cow pony, and threw her arms in the air. "You finally did come like you promised. Oh, Slocum, I nearly gave up. I didn't think you'd ever be able to get me out."

"Yes, let's go!"

"Oh, yes," she shouted. "I can't believe we're getting away."

"Me either, but we are. Ride, girl." She sounded sensible enough to him. He acted exactly like that when he got out of prisons and jails—couldn't get enough free air. Maybe she wasn't crazy after all—thank God.

He planned to take her to Paso, and let Goldfarb help him find a place for her to stay. They raced their horses across the oyster-white desert beyond the ditches and small fields, a small slice of the moon rising over Madres.

They reached Paso in two days. They reined up in front of the mercantile and hitched their horses. Slocum gave a critical look around the sleepy village—siesta time—and motioned for her to go inside. No sign that any of the scalpers or the *federales* were about, but he couldn't be careful enough.

"Amigo!" Goldfarb shouted, and came forward, a great smile on his smooth face.

"Goldfarb, this is Lucia Sallisar," he said.

The man took her hand and kissed her fingers, then genuflected before he straightened. "My pleasure, my lovely lady."

"Yes, thank you," she said as if flustered by his attention.

"She needs some clothing. Her wardrobe has been delayed," Slocum said as she stood with her arms folded and turned away from the man.

"I understand. Ruby, come assist this young lady, please?" He turned and bowed his head. "My wife will be glad to show you suitable clothing."

"Thanks," she said, then gave Slocum a private head shake before Ruby led her off, babbling away about men and how inconsiderate they were at times.

He even heard Lucia laugh at the woman's words. Good, she would recover in time. He could hardly escape the vision of the girl's ripe body and beauty. Even when she was dressed in the simple cotton shift, her appeal took away his breath.

"You have been absent too long, my amigo," Goldfarb said as he broke into his train of thoughts.

"Oh, I've been in jail and been to the mountains with that bloody McVain."

"Allow me to secure us a good bottle of spirits and we shall go upstairs to share it, and you can tell me all about your adventures."

When he finished telling Goldfarb about all of his deeds and problems, both men were settled in chairs looking out the open French doors on to the patio below.

"McVain is not a man to desert. Secondly, you know he will hate you for spoiling his raid."

"Tough."

"You will need to be extra careful, for I am certain that Sallisar will sent his *pistoleros* out after you for kidnapping his daughter from the convent."

"I guess all those sisters at the mission were very old as she described them. So I was fortunate because they slept through my noisy breakout. I could still see one of them with a shotgun ordering me and her to get back inside."

Both men laughed.

"The Apaches need supplies," Goldfarb finally said. "I can hardly offer them sanctuary here with McVain on the move, the Mexican Army moving troops close by south of here, and reports of the American forces coming into the mountains."

"So what do you plan?"

"A pack train is possible." The man leaned back, tented his pink-skinned fingers on top of his massive girth, and stared at Slocum.

"You keep looking at me like I could do something."

"Only man I know could get one in and to them."

"Then I would be in trouble with all the authorities both here and at home."

"Being in trouble, as you call it, is not something new, I take it from your past escapades."

"Yes, but taking supplies to hostiles past both McVain and two armies might be more than even a ghost could do."

Goldfarb shrugged his thick shoulders under the silk gown. "Some men feast on adventure and a challenge. Slocum, you are such a person."

"What's in it for me?"

"Oh, two hundred American. Does that sound generous enough?"

"Plenty generous. The question is simply enough, could I live long enough to enjoy it."

"Then it's settled?"

"I've not said I would go."

"I'll pay you the two hundred now so you can enjoy it immediately."

Slocum shook his head at the offer. He was grateful that Lucia had come up the stairs dressed in a brown riding outfit, a canvas skirt that embraced her slender hips, a white blouse, and short-waisted jacket.

"You look much better and more comfortable," he said as he rose and offered her a chair.

"I would think so," she said, accepting the seat and smiling at him.

"What will you do now?" Goldfarb asked her directly.

"Since my father considers me insane, I guess I will run around as a madwoman."

Both men laughed aloud.

"You are most welcome to stay here until you decided where you wish to live," Goldfarb said.

"Thank you. I really have no idea what to do next."

"That will be good," Slocum said. "I am taking a pack train into the Madres and may be gone for a week or so. You'll be safe enough here until I return."

"Yes. However, I must warn you that my father may send some of his *pistoleros* after me."

"If you remain in my house, I don't believe any locals will tell them where you are," Goldfarb said.

"Good, line up some good men with mules and load them," Slocum said. "I plan to be on my way by daybreak."

He read some kind of silent protest about his leaving in Lucia's face, but he dismissed it when she smiled at him instead. She'd be safe inside the compound. When he returned, maybe he would take her north to Arizona. Tucson society needed a pretty face and slender hips like hers to turn men's gazes; he could set her up and arrange for her to meet someone suitable to marry. Anyway, one day she would be heir to a great hacienda—yes, he would do that after the pack-train drive.

Dawn came over the Madres. He was ready to lead the train of braying mules up the high trail. The bolder he acted about the pack train, the less likely he was to draw attention. Each packer carried a pistol and a hundred rounds of ammunition. Several, who were better shots and understood their operation, carried Winchesters as well. A total of eighteen men were going along. Many were in their teens but they knew the dangers and looked flush-faced with the excitement in the lantern light while they loaded the animals.

"What do you think, Sanchez?" he asked his head packer.

"We are ready, señor." The man was experienced; he rode a short-legged mountain pony about the courtyard and urged the workers to hurry.

When they began to move out on the road, Slocum rode a leggy gray horse from Goldfarb's stables up and down the line. The barb-bred horse held an arch in his neck; his small ears flecked about to listen and point his attention. A long unruly mane rose and spilled over the right side. The horse stepped out with an unexpectedly smooth running walk that pleased Slocum.

He encouraged the packers as they scolded the mules into line. One mule, marked with lots of white coloration, brayed in protest as a young boy jerked with both hands on the lead.

"He looks like he don't want to go?" Slocum quizzed the obvious youngster under the poncho and straw hat.

"I'll get him," the boy said in a hoarse voice from under his wide-brimmed straw hat, and never looked up at Slocum, so intent was he on making the animal obey.

To help the determined packer, Slocum rode in close and whacked the mule on the rump. It surged forward, but the youth recovered very quickly and grapped for his hat.

"*Gracias,*" the boy said, never looking back, coughing as he hurried away with his mule.

Something was familiar about the young packer, but Slocum could not say what it was. He shrugged off the matter and rode on. There was plenty to worry about besides a single boy and a paint mule.

Stranger than that only Ruth and Goldfarb had seen him off. Lucia must have finally fallen deep asleep, though he had no idea how she had managed through all the noise and confusion of the packing. It was no secret to anyone within hearing, and he felt certain even the Apaches had heard them in the mountains.

Perhaps if all went well, in few days he would be returning with Goldfarb's proceeds and could collect his own two hundred American. He wouldn't let the man pay him until he returned successfully. A dollar had to be earned, he figured.

"We are on the way, Sanchez," he said to the older man who headed the line on his bay.

The short wiry Mexican removed his high sombrero and

wiped his face on his sleeve. "Ah, *sí*, Slocum, we are on the way. But I wish the padre had come and blessed us before we left."

"Where was he?"

Sanchez shrugged, and then he shouted to one of the boys to make one of his mules walk faster. Slocum sent the gray into a long trot. He wanted to scout the way up the narrow canyon confines for any sign of an ambush. He felt clean after the bath and shave the night before. All set to get filthy again, he mused as he rode ahead.

Had she been so deep asleep she had not awakened to wave good-bye? He tried to dismiss her absence. Besides, what did he have to offer such a beautiful girl? No, it was better she'd stayed. If anything happened to him on this trip, then Goldfarb would care for her. It was better that way—he rose in the stirrups and scouted the canyon walls above the trail. Chances were good that he would never see an ambush until they struck, but he still searched the towering bluffs.

He short-loped the gray up the canyon and, standing in the stirrups on the final steep path, he came out on top. He searched the scene where the scalpers had once posted guard—no sign of anyone except cold ashes—then he carefully studied the bridge across the sky. If he didn't lose a silly mule or two getting them across it, he would consider himself lucky.

He leaned an elbow on the big saddlehorn and stuck a quirlie in his mouth. Then cupping a lucifer he'd struck alive on a concho, slowly he drew on the cylinder of tobacco. The rich smoke filled his mouth as he considered the crossing and inhaled deeply. The tobacco settled him as the cool wind swept his face.

The gray took a mincing step onto the narrow catwalk across the ridgeback. Slocum wanted to slap the horse and impress on the animal the seriousness of the thin trail. No time for fancy footwork—it was thousands of feet to one's death off either side. Then as if on cue, the horse dropped his head and sniffed the path. Each step measured and sure, head low as if sighting his next move, he began the journey on many such measured movements.

Tiny grains of gravel spilled away from the sides, traced off a few yards, gained momentum, then flew to the unseen ground far beneath them. There was no place to stumble or turn, one was committed once one began the journey toward the timbered slopes perhaps a mile away.

A time for him to sit tall in the saddle and fill his lungs with thin mountain air, ready like a cat should anything upset the horse's equilibrium beneath him. He listened to the whine of the wind in his ears and the surging of blood from his heart. It was a place for him to repeatedly dry the sticky sweat from his palms despite the cool mountain air. He was on a tightrope up where eagles flew and there were no rails to prevent his fall.

The black-timbered slopes grew closer; he studied them for any sign of opposition. Great cumulus clouds began to build; by afternoon they would have showers somewhere in the mountains. He hoped his train was across before the showers began. He glanced back. No sign of the pack animals. They would be hours yet coming up the canyon. Far to the north and south, the hazy face of the Madres rose to greet him.

"Easy, horse," he spoke softly.

18

"Señor, will the Apaches find us?" Sanchez asked.

"There is a valley perhaps a half a day from here. If there is no military or scalpers nearby, they will meet us there, I'd bet."

Slocum drank coffee from the tin cup and let the cold morning wind sweep his face. It was almost dawn on the second day, and so far the trip had been uneventful; two days on the march and they had seen nothing, though he felt certain the Apaches had checked on them. Once he saw the flash of horse turning on a hillside, another a quick picture of a bandanna-bound head peering down from among some large rocks. The Chiricahuas knew they were coming.

"What will you do when this is over?" Sanchez asked.

"Go back north. My welcome is about worn out down here with those trumped-up charges about me stealing the ring from the Sallisars."

"It must be nice to see so much country all the time."

"Do you miss your wife and little ones?" Slocum asked the man.

"Oh, *sí*, I think of them all the time."

"So do I, only I don't have any to go back to."

"It is said you must walk in a man's sandals before you really want to trade places with him."

Slocum agreed. Then he went for the gray horse; one of the packers had already saddled it for him and stood holding it. He had to admit that Sanchez saw to his comfort, and he appreciated his concern to watch the horse closely since it was no ordinary animal.

He thanked the man when he took the reins and then mounted. The mules were braying loud enough to make four choruses. Some even tried to buck as the packers proceeded to saddle them. Occasionally one jerked loose, and three or so packers circled the animal with arms spread out to deflect it until the lead shank could be re-caught.

Slocum paused on the rise above the camp to overlook the pack train, and then wheeled the big horse around. He needed to find this valley and plan the placement of what he hoped would be his final camp and trade center.

The small stream teemed with darting silver trout as he let the gray drink deep. With plenty of grass for the mules, the stream bottom would be an ideal place to set up. He rode off on the hillside; there he tied the gray's reins to his front leg so he could graze and wouldn't stray far.

Satisfied he was alone, he stretched out on his back and took a short siesta.

Something told him he wasn't alone when he awoke. How long had he been asleep? Three riders sat with rifles over their laps and no hats not twenty yards from him. They waited for him.

"Howdy," he drawled, sitting up and combing his hair. No sense acting like a crazy man. They had time to kill him if they had wanted to. He wasn't as clever as he thought sneaking a thirty-minute nap.

"Where is Gatewood and Horn?" the Apache who acted as leader asked.

"They killed Crawford," Slocum said. "Gatewood ain't here. Horn took Crawford's body back." He had no idea where the lieutenant was.

"Geronimo is going to meet Nantan Lupan."

"Oh," he said, still not certain how that worked. "To surrender?"

"Yes. We want to speak to Gatewood and Horn. They

have lived among us. We don't know these others.''

Slocum considered how they had not spoken of Crawford. He had lived among them. Why didn't they acknowledge his death? Then he recalled that the Apaches did not talk of the dead—bad business. They wanted a living person, not a dead man. Somehow they looked like children to him, despite their hawk noses, eyes hard as diamonds, and no telling how many men, women and children they had killed. They wanted leadership at this time—*they followed many leaders*. Natise's words rang like a bell.

There were many clans in the Apache nation; many hated the other branches as badly as the Pima and Papagos hated the Apache. To send all the bands to San Carlos was like mixing mad bulls in the first place. Hunters were told to stand in line for bad flour and wormy beans. To be counted and wear numbers, to be ordered to stop making *tiswain*, their own concoction for liquor made from the century plant roots. Why, Crook even made them stop cutting off the noses of their unfaithful women. How could a man tell one when he saw one if she wasn't plainly marked?

He rose to his feet. ''Are your people going to this surrender?''

''If we can talk to someone we trust. We want to go back, but not without guns to protect our families from our enemies.''

''Chiricahuas have many enemies,'' he agreed. ''Will others come here? I have a large train of goods from Paso— from Goldfarb to trade.''

Hell, if Geronimo was planing to surrender, perhaps Slocum was too late to trade with them. They might all be drawing out to go back to the reservation.

''They will come,'' the leader announced, and turned his horse about.

''If I see Horn, what should I tell him?'' Slocum shouted after them.

''He needs to come talk to us.''

''Who? I mean, who should he come look for?''

''His wife's people.''

''Sure,'' Slocum said, knowing that Horn had once had

an Apache wife and lived with the band near Cibeque Creek on the reservation.

Slocum had more to concern him. If the Apaches did come, would they buy enough to cover Goldfarb's costs? He hoped so as he slapped on his hat and headed for the stream to get a drink. Geronimo was going to give up. Hard to believe. The blasted mountains were nearly impenetrable; the Mexicans couldn't root him out—they wouldn't try. Why, they hired killers like McVain and supplied him with felons to fight them. Where was the Highlander? He hoped a million leagues away, but he probably wasn't far. Slocum needed to get his trading complete and headed back to Paso quick as he could.

A few hours later the obvious noise of the mule train came into hearing. Slocum walked out to greet them and spoke to Sanchez.

"We made it this far in good shape," Slocum said. "You've done a good job."

"*Gracias*, but what about the Apaches, señor?"

"They've been here. A few of them came by earlier. They told me a strange thing, Sanchez. They said that Geronimo was going to surrender but that they would come and trade with us."

"Surrender to who? I have heard the Alocade in Fronterous has been sending word to them that he would sign a peace treaty with them."

"No, this man said he would surrender to Crook and the Americans."

"Maybe the fox plays both sides for the best terms?"

"He may do that. Let's put out things in a neat order in the center out here and post some guards around our camp. Not someone that's trigger-happy either."

"I will pick men to do that. Some of those boys could not hit a mountain and might do as you say, shoot first."

"I don't want any friendly ones shot at." He hoped he'd made his point clear. They were in no position to have a mixup and have to go to fighting.

"We will picket the gray, señor."

"Good," Slocum said, and headed for the stream. He

planned to find a place where he could take a bath and not be disturbed. En route he circled the men busy off-loading the panniers and stacking the goods. Down through the willows, he finally found a place suitably screened by the brush for privacy. Seated on his butt, he began removing his boots, then his gun belt, vest, the leather pants, and then his shirt.

Testing the water, he felt the chill of the snow source, and knew it would be cold. With a deep inhale, he plowed into the pool and then dove into the clear surface, stroking for the far side.

He rose to wipe the water from his eyes and push the wet hair from his face. Someone else had the same intention. The boy who had struggled with the paint mule had removed his pants, then his wide hat, and the dark fall of black hair forced him to blink. This was no boy. She swept the vest and blouse off her head, and there was no missing her pear-shaped breasts before she dove into the pool. Lucia!

"You should never leave a woman without asking her if she wants to come along," she said, rising up, water streaming from her smooth skin, and wading toward him.

"How did you hide in that camp of boys?" he asked.

"They thought I was just bashful," she said, and stood with her hands on her hips before him. Beads of water glistened on her smooth skin.

"I think you better—" he began.

"No, you've avoided me long enough."

"Avoided you? I was sent to retrieve you."

"Am I ugly? Too fat?" She held her arms out for him to examine her.

"Oh, hell, no!"

"Then do something about it." Her eyes narrowed as she defied him.

Slocum nodded slowly as he considered the shapely body before him. "Yes, ma'am, I will."

19

"The Apaches are here," she whispered. Her firm breast pressed against him as he tried to consider the hour. It was near dawn. An orange edge on the top of the timber line above them told him a lot about the hour as his palm rode down the silky curve of her back and then he cupped her butt. She wiggled against him and the tip of her tongue sought his ear.

"Aren't you afraid of them?" she whispered.

"At this moment that is as far from my mind—"

"Well, we better get up. We can't do this all day."

"That's negotiable."

She rolled away from him, pulling up the blankets to conceal her nakedness. "It certainly isn't with this place bristling with Chiricahuas." On her back she began to pull on her britches under the covers.

"What if Tomatoes comes?"

She hesitated. "Do I need to decide? I mean, do I have any choices?"

"I can take you to Tucson. I have some friends in high places that could find you a suitable husband."

"Would he believe I was a virgin?"

"I did."

She pounded him in the upper arm with her fist and set her lips in a tight line before she went back to dressing.

"Men excuse beautiful women for their indiscretions," he added.

She shook her head, then quickly pulled the blouse over her head. "I don't know, after I have been with the Apaches and ridden my butt off with you, if I could be Mrs. Tea Party and what society wants."

"Perhaps a rancher's wife."

"What would that be like?"

"You could ride and rope with him."

"Would a man let me do that?" She hugged her knees and looked across the pine-forested slopes as if in deep thought about all the possibilities.

"How the hell could he not let you?" The only man who couldn't see her beauty was her father. It was stupid for him to lose his only child, but some men never learned that their daughters did not always bend to their mold.

"Maybe," she said, tying the rope she used for a belt as she stood above him. "The best idea is to take me to El Paso and I can work as a *puta*."

"Suit yourself," he said, flinging the covers back to pull on his pants. She frowned in disapproval at his nakedness, and turned her head.

Finally dressed, he stomped off in his boots for some coffee. Sanchez met him before he reached the large campfire.

"One of the packers is gone. He was very quiet and no one knew much about him."

"I know." Slocum yawned and lazily stretched his arms over his head. "He came and slept with me last night."

"Oh—" The head packer's eyes widened in alarm.

"It wasn't a boy." He knew by the man's shocked appearance he had not known who she was. Slocum lowered his voice, "It was Lucia Sallisar."

"The Don's daughter?"

"Yes, we better trade for a horse from the Apaches for her to ride back."

"She was the boy with the paint mule?" Sanchez removed his sombrero and scratched his scalp.

"She fooled all of us, huh?"

"Wait till I tell the men."

"Don't tell them. Let them guess how she got up here."

Both men laughed out loud. Slocum went for their coffee.

Natise had ridden in with the first ones. Slocum saw him about an hour after he had gotten up. A smaller version of Cochise, Natise looked almost too young to be a chief of his people. He was hardly five-three or five-four, while his father had towered over most men. Natise stood apart as the women packed off sacks of flour and beans to stack nearby.

Slocum crossed to where he stood.

"Has the chief of the Chiricahuas decided to go back to San Carlos?" he asked openly.

Natise shook his head. "Bad rumors, some will go back. There is no need. We would not have guns, no *tiswain*, our women would become like wild dogs."

"Wild dogs?"

"Yes, there would be no way to teach them better things."

"You mean you could not beat them?"

"I mean they would do as they please."

"But they say that Geronimo is going to surrender."

"He is one leader."

"I see. Goldfarb has sent many things for you and your people to trade for." He indicated the piled store goods; he wanted the man to know that his employer had tried to serve him and the others.

"Tell him, he tells the truth," Natise said. "Not many tell us truths. But soon the Mexicans will tire of losing men in the mountains and the soldiers will go back like before. Americans will go home too. This is not their land."

"You have it all figured out?" Slocum asked.

Natise agreed with a bob of his head. "Chiricahuas were here before the first Mexicans came. Once we lived in peace with them, but they did not like Indians who did not come and work for them."

"So?"

"So they poisoned us and tried to trap us. We have been at war since before my grandfather walked this land."

"So you have been at war. Will you continue to fight?"

"Yes! I intend to die in this land."

"That could very well happen," Slocum said, carefully measuring the man's resolve.

"Americans, Mexicans, scalpers, they will pay dear for my life."

"I am certain they will."

Natise spat in the dust. "They will."

Slocum gave him a salute and turned to leave.

"What have they done with Horn and Gatewood?" the chief asked.

Slocum paused and turned back to face the chief. "I don't think Gatewood is not stationed any longer in Arizona. Horn is somewhere around." He made a waving gesture with his hand.

Natise acknowledged he had heard him. The chieftain had made up his mind: stay and die if necessary. Some would follow him for he was heir-apparent chief. Slocum turned and went to help the men with the trading. Three of the packers were store clerks. But the rest were just farm boys, and no doubt in the thick of things he could help.

He wondered if Lucia had stayed away from the center of trade and out of sight. She obviously had a mind of her own to hide as a boy among the men for two days and do it successfully. Bashful. He wanted to laugh at her words, recalling the pleasures of her body.

More Apaches shifted in. He began to feel that his mission might be a success. Two hundred American was good wages for this job—the money would see him and the girl to Arizona as well as finance her introduction to society. She might give up the *puta* notion when she drew the attention of a handsome young man. Hell, she could always do that if she hated her life and fell out of a husband-wife relationship.

He knew the next man who rode at the head of the column. The hard chiseled features of the little man the mere

mention of whose name froze blood in people's veins—
Geronimo.

"Slocum—we meet again," Geronimo said, his hand
close to the butt of his Colt. His diamond-hard eyes bored
a hole in Slocum. He held his rifle in his other hand, his
obvious distrust written on his dark oaken face as he halted
the horse with only knee pressure.

"I am here for Goldfarb," Slocum said. "I am here as
a friend of Chiricahuas."

Geronimo looked over the piles of store goods. "You
are here to trade for gold, is that not so?"

"That's how he buys more goods."

"My band will need no more than you buy. We go to
meet Nantan Lupan."

"I have heard that, but there are others who wish to
stay."

"What would you do? You are a white man and you do
not ride the road."

"You saying I'm careful?" Slocum asked.

"No! I say you are like the Apache. You too hide from
the authorities like the marshal in Tucson."

"You better not surrender to him."

Geronimo nodded, then dismounted on the right side and
switched the new Winchester in his right hand. "I will tell
Nantan Lupan that I surrender to him and the blue coats,
not that law?"

"Did you come to tell me or ask me?"

"Where are the scalpers?" He looked around as if
checking.

"I haven't seen them in ten days."

"I owe you for the lives of my band. Only one white
man would have stolen an Apache horse and rode him away
like that."

"The horse was payment enough."

Gernimo frowned at the approach of a rider. He tossed
his head for Slocum to turn and see who was coming.

"Where is she?" A tall Apache sighted menacingly

down the barrel of his repeater at Slocum's heart. The rifle's butt plate was jammed into the buck's shoulder and a brown finger was curled around the trigger. Slocum considered his options. Death looked a hair's breadth away.

20

Geronimo strode over and looked up at the man with the rifle. "If you kill him, then perhaps you will find this woman. But he came to my camp and saved many sleeping woman and children from the scalpers' army. His heart is brave for a white man."

"Where is the woman Lucia?" the big man shouted as if he had not heard a word the other leader had passed on. Then Tomatoes kicked out of the stirrups and bounded from his horse like an athlete. The rifle looked like a small stick in his hand as he advanced on Slocum.

"You certain she wants to be your woman?" Slocum asked, looking the powerful man up and down. If there was an ounce of fat on the burly form, he wondered what crease it was concealed in.

"I did not ask you. Where have you hid her?" He waved the rifle around like it weighed nothing.

"She can make up her own mind. Besides, she told me you have a wife in Arizona."

Tomatoes frowned and stopped. "She thinks that?"

"She is very proud. Her people are chiefs in this land. She does not wish to share even a man as powerful as you are with another woman."

"Where is she?" He scowled at the trading and searched about with a pained expression.

146

"You don't think she's here, do you?"

"No, but she is not at her father's ranch. Nor at the place where they said she was—the church place with the mothers in black."

He had been on her trail too. How did an Apache manage so much travel and know so much? They had ways. He needed to calm the young man down and send him on his way—she had not indicated that she had chosen him, despite his questions. No doubt this bull of an Apache was a he-man, enough to make any young woman faint-hearted. The lingering problem was this other wife, near as he could figure it out.

"They said that someone took her." Tomatoes stood on his toes and surveyed the crowd of women and children busy marketing with their men. "Was it you?"

"Would I bring her here if I had?"

"She left my camp with you."

"I was paid to return her to her father."

"He is the fool who sent her to the church prison?"

Slocum agreed, satisfied the big Chiricahua was sufficiently defused to go on his way. Geronimo too had seen the danger pass away between them, and had gone to look at the trade goods.

Away from the hostile chieftain, Slocum surveyed the trading and saw things were in hand. What would she do? He was in camp looking for her. At the counter made from stacked crates, Sanchez oversaw the young man who weighted the gold dust the Apaches paid in. A line of shoppers stood patiently with goods piled about them as the process of paying out went from family to family.

They looked tired, their clothing dirty from an obvious lack of time or facilities to launder them. He recalled the proud Chiricahuas when they were at the Jeffords agency. The women all strutted around in clean dresses, and many skirts swirled around their shapely brown ankles. In those days he had danced and drunk *tiswain* with some of the divorced ones, and even considered taking one of the special ones for his bride.

These people's eyes were sunk deep in their heads, their

mouths drawn too tight to smile. No one flirted; they spoke to their children sharply as if their childish ways were a threat to the entire tribe.

That was it! Slocum had not heard any laughter—not one of the women giggled with another one this trading day. He realized Geronimo had seen and heard all this—time to go back, no matter the losses. They were dead on their feet, pushed so hard by the armies of both countries.

"Slo-cum!"

He turned at the call. Something clinked as it struck at his feet, and his gaze fell on the small sack that Geronimo had tossed.

"I wish to hire you."

"For what?" Slocum asked.

"Go find Tom Horn. Tell him to meet us at the Place of the Skull. We will be there in five days to surrender."

"Send an Apache."

"No, you go find him!"

"Keep your money."

"No. You do not know where the yellow gold comes from the ground. Take it. I will not need it when I go back to the reservation. You will, for you have no reservation to stay on."

"I'll have to look for Horn. He may not be anywhere close."

"He once lived with us. He does not lie to us."

"Give me ten days." He held up his fingers.

Geronimo agreed. He stood with his arms folded waiting; then he nodded in approval when Slocum swept up the pouch. He jammed it in his waistband and headed for their campfire. He needed something to wash down all that had happened. Was she out of sight? Damn strange the Apaches knew so much and didn't see through her disguise—luck was all.

He had a cup of thick left-over coffee in a cup when Natise rode up to him and reined up. "These men would never have come here without you to guard them."

"One man?" Slocum asked with a grin.

"They would be wetting their pants to come in these

mountains and deal with us. You are a great sign to them.''

"*Gracias*," Slocum said to the man's compliment.

"This one who wears the woman's skirt?''

"McVain?''

"Yes, he is the one. Someday we will meet and I will stake him on an anthill after I cut out his manhood.''

Slocum just nodded that he understood as he considered the coffee. Then he spotted one of the packers under his blankets with a sombrero over his face. It was Lucia. Did Natise see her, or did he think it only a boy sick and sleeping?

Slocum tasted the coffee, then walked to the chief. "I'd have killed him myself but the opportunity did not come. I better check on Sanchez.''

Natise whirled his horse and loped north away from the campfire and trading grounds. The Apaches were leaving like smoke, soon to disappear in the pines and behind the boulders. Slocum saw that their business in the mountains was completed. Sanchez was locking the receipts in a strongbox.

"I forgot.'' Sanchez motioned for him to come closer. "I never asked for that horse that you needed for her. I apologize.''

Slocum looked over the exhausted men that lounged around, and grinned. "Damn good thing you never mentioned it.''

Sanchez dropped heavily to a crate and sighed in relief. "All we have to do is go home. What did Geronimo want from you?''

"He hired me to go find Tom Horn.''

"That American scout that came through with the officer's body?''

"Yes, I wonder wherever the hell he's at?'' Slocum shook his head—his days to complete the task were numbered.

Sanchez threw up his hands, showing his pale palms. He obviously didn't know.

"Don't mention my 'boy' either.''

The *segundo* slapped his knees and laughed out loud. "What do we do next?"

"We sleep a few hours and move out at midnight. When the sun comes up, I want us at the Devil's Crossing."

"If we can cross there, we can make it home safely," Sanchez agreed.

"Yes. We better post guards tonight; there are still enemies in the land."

"*Sí.*"

He left the man and strolled off to find a place to bathe. It would be many days before he had another chance riding from hell to breakfast looking for Horn. No telling where the scout might be but, Fort Huchuca might be the best place to look, and that was a hundred miles north or more after he got out of the mountains.

"Pst," she hissed at him from the cover of a large juniper.

"Oh," he said without looking. "A big man was here today looking for you. Said he wanted to marry you."

"That sumbitch!" she swore from her concealment. "He wants more damn wives than one of them Mormons."

"Stay out of sight," he said in a loud whisper. "He may have scouts watching us. Why didn't you tell me he was so big?" Slocum tried to look like a man thinking out something alone in case he was being watched.

"He is big, ain't he?"

"What I saw was big." He walked on, chuckling to himself, and heard her hiss "You bastard" after him.

When it was dark, he called her out of hiding and handed her a plate of beans and a cup of coffee. He sat cross-legged on the ground opposite her and listened to the whippoorwills calling in the night. Starlight cast long shadows on the grassy ground.

"We're leaving at midnight for the Crossing. After that you and I are riding for Paso. You can stay there—"

"Where are you going?" Her dark eyes flashed in the night.

"I have to ride like hell and find Tom Horn for Geronimo. He paid me today to go do that." He drew the pouch out and counted the coins. They came close to a hundred American. Payment enough for the job.

"I can ride like hell," she said, breaking his thoughts. "You're my ticket out of this country and I intend to be a burr in your tail."

"It ain't—"

"No place for a woman. I know what you're going to say, but forget it." She pointed the spoon at him. "I drove five of those stubborn mules up here and those boys didn't know I was a girl."

"I knew it the first day when I saw you struggling with that paint mule."

"No, you never did such a thing."

"I told Sanchez that you were a boy when he worried one was missing and you were sleeping with me."

"You don't do such things, do you?"

"You don't know what I do. You stay at Paso with Gold-farb while I'm gone."

"And have my father's *pistoleros* drag me back home? No!" She stamped her foot.

Somehow he would have to convince her that he was right. He looked at the first flood of the moon as it started to cross the high top of the mountain. The crescent half-circle would last until dawn. All he needed the extra light for was to guide his pack train to the crossing.

Midnight and the mountains echoed with the protest of the mules. He shook his head as he walked from one end to the other of the train. A disapproving scream of an angry animal cut the darkness, then the sound of sharp hooves connecting with a solid kick followed, by the resounding complaint of the packer who cursed the mule's relatives for ten centuries. Slocum worried they would tell anyone in earshot that he was moving out. Most of the trade goods had been sold, which meant they should travel quicker go-ing than coming. Plus the mules would soon savvy they were headed for home, and the packers would have to hold them back.

He took the reins from Lucia and mounted the gray. Then he reached down and pulled her up behind on top of his bedroll. She adjusted herself.

"Ready," she said softly.

He booted the gray out into a long walk. They passed the busy packers fussing with their stock, and he rode up to Sanchez.

"Ready?" he asked the man.

"*Sí*, señor." Sanchez touched his high-crown hat for her and smiled in the moonlight that gleamed on his straight teeth. "God bless you little one."

She waved to indicate that she'd heard him; then she reached to grab Slocum with her other hand and save her seat as he set the gray on his way. Settled in, she buried her face in his shirt as she laughed and they rode out ahead of the column.

"You told him that I was that boy and I slept with you?"

"That's my very words."

"I've ruined someone else's reputation huh?"

"Sure did." He could see a distant wing of the mountains far to the north glowing in the lunar light. Somewhere beyond the next range or further, Tom Horn was either raising hell with a couple of whores in some saloon, or sleeping rolled up in a blanket in some dry wash with a handful of Apache scouts. His next job was to settle Lucia someplace and get on with his search for him.

21

"You can't convince her to stay?" Goldfarb asked as he handed Slocum the pouch with the two hundred dollars.

Slocum looked across the courtyard in the long shadows of pre-dawn. Already mounted, Lucia held the leads to the other two saddled horses. He shook his head in disgust as he studied her dressed in the fresh new clothing, sitting the horse astride and ready to ride. He had tried his damnedest—she wasn't about to be tricked or left behind despite his threat they would ride their horses into the ground that day.

"Good luck, my friend." Goldfarb said as they shook hands.

For a long moment, a knot formed in Slocum's throat. A strange feeling of premonition crept over him. He didn't want to leave his friend or ride north to find Horn. Something was wrong in this place—he seldom had such a notion of such pending doom.

"You keep up your guard while I'm gone," he said. "McVain or the Mexican army might learn about your business and I don't want anything to happen to you and Ruby or the people in the village. They're brave men among them."

"Don't worry about us, we will be fine. Hurry back, amigo."

Slocum grasped the horn in both hands and swung himself up. He wished he felt as certain as the big man sounded. Nothing he could do but ride. He waved to Ruby on the porch and Sanchez, who stood ready to open the courtyard gate for them.

"Come on, woman, we got miles to make," he said as Lucia smiled to the others and shouted good-bye.

They set heels to their mounts; each led an extra saddled horse, to change back and forth to as they drove north. It was well over a hundred miles to Huachuca, and there was no time for them to talk with their horses in a full gallop. The cool air of morning flowed over his smooth-shaven face as they swept past the farmland and into the desert. After ten miles of hard riding, each leading their own spare, their mounts were short of breath and shoulders soaked in sweat, and he told her to change to her other horse on the run. He watched to be certain that she could do it. The stretch he chose was smooth and he knew held the least danger for her.

"Yes!" he shouted with pride at her easy maneuver to the second horse; then he swapped horses himself and lashed the fresh mount into a faster pace. They had miles to cover and it might require more horseflesh, but he intended to find Horn as quickly as possible if he hadn't left the country.

In the afternoon they paused to water their horses at a small ranchero. The man's pregnant wife apologized that there was no goat meat to eat as she served them beans and tortillas. The coyotes had thinned her small herd and her man had promised to buy her more. Under the scrutiny of four wide-eyed naked children, they ate their food in silence beneath the palm-frond-roofed *remada*. He felt proud Lucia had not once asked him how much further they must ride. Though she looked tired, she remained stiff-backed and as determined-looking as ever when he told her they needed to quickly move on.

When they finished their meal and cinched up their horses, Slocum paid the rancher's wife a few dollars "to buy some goats with." She protested, but he indicated the children and then her distended belly. "Buy goats for them."

At that she agreed with a grin to accept the money, and waved after him. He heard her tell the children, *He buys you goats*. They shouted and ran after the two of them screaming things like, *May the Virgin bless you*.

"Even if you sleep with boys, you're a good man!" Lucia shouted, riding stirrup to stirrup with him.

"Don't tell that to too many," he screamed back over the thunder of hooves.

Long past midnight, they reached Fort Huachuca on completely jaded horses in a walk. Slocum knew they had made nearly a hundred miles since the dawn cracked in Paso, and had ridden their horses into the ground. A black sentry stood in the lamplight outside the orderly building. He halted Slocum at the steps.

"You have business here, sir?"

"I need to find the whereabouts of Tom Horn, the civilian scout."

"He won't be in there," the buffalo soldier said.

"You know where Tom is?"

"He be up in Tombstone tonight, seeing them bright lights and be riding that elephant, sir."

"Tom can do that, can't he, soldier?"

The private stood up at attention and said "Yes sir" as he shouldered his weapon.

"Who are you?" a voice of authority asked from the doorway.

Slocum turned. "A friend of Tom Horn's and a man with information that Horn needs about the hostiles."

A stiff-backed West Point shavetail stood above them. Slocum had known a thousand of them. The lieutenant shoved out his chest. "I am the officer in charge here. Anything you have for a scout of this man's army you can report to me."

"Pardon, sir, but my message is for Horn. But if you could provide a conveyance *for my wife* and me up to Tombstone so we could tell Tom this information sooner?"

"Excuse my manner, ma'am," the officer said and swept

off his hat, not realizing the rider was not a man up to that point. "Lieutenant Jack Pershing."

She nodded she'd heard him, sitting slump-shouldered in the saddle.

"That's Mrs. Slocum," Slocum said to the man in a form of introduction. "We've come a long ways on a very important mission."

"Slocum, I will have your horses stabled and a dray brought up for you. Your wife looks very tired. Could I offer the lady a room while you complete this mission?"

Slocum walked around beside her left stirrup to convince her she needed to stay there. He reached her leg and looked up when she fainted away. In a tumble she fell out of the saddle into his arms.

"I believe she wants to accept your generous offer, Pershing." He stood holding her limp form in his arms.

Pershing looked aghast at Slocum and his armful of sprawled-out woman. The officer finally said, "Follow me. She will be perfectly safe in my quarters until you return, sir."

"I certainly hope so," Slocum said, giving her a boost to better carry her. "When we have her in your bunk, may I borrow a horse to ride up there?"

"Certainly. Private, go saddle my horse Boots for Mr. Slocum."

Good name. It described Lucia. She was as tough as boots. However, he should have realized that long a day would do her in. The dozen miles or so left to Tombstone would go quickly on a fresh horse—then he would have to locate Tom. He looked down as her eyes opened in slits to look up at him.

"You'll be fine, darling," Slocum said. "The lieutenant says you'll be safe in his quarters until I can return."

She nodded and closed her eyes, too weary to protest.

In the early morning hour before dawn, Tombstone was still wide-open when Slocum rode the Lieutenant's high-headed gelding up Allen Street. Despite the time of night, the tinny piano music carried into the street and the free laughter of whores rang like bells to his ears.

"Hey, buster, get off that damn horse and come climb on me," a lady of the night shouted to him. She swung on the porch post of the saloon in her low-cut satin gown.

He reined the horse in close and looked her over in the yellow light streaming out of the saloon's doors.

"You seen Tom Horn tonight?" he asked.

"Seen him—hell, I'd jumped his bones, if I'd seen him." Her words were whiskey-slurred as she stepped off the porch to approach him. She patted his leg familiarly and looked up as if dazed by the effects of too much to drink.

"Thanks. I may be back," he said, easing the big black back from her.

"I can damn sure handle you!" she shouted after him. "Ask for Sally—do!"

He waved a hand to show he'd heard her as he pushed down the street. Four saloons later, he learned that Tom had been at the Bird Cage the last time anyone had heard from him.

Slocum rode to the adobe structure on the end of the block, but the hitch rack was crowded, so he was forced to go to the side to hitch the horse to a mesquite tree with several others. Every male in Cochise County must be in town. Strange, it was usually miners frequenting the bars, but at this late hour—who could say.

"Tom Horn," he said to the bartender in the lobby. He slapped a silver dollar down to pay for his information.

The tall dark-eyed man with a heavy mustache tossed his head toward the west set of stairs. "He's with Lucy in the third crib, up them stairs. But I'd advise you wait here till he comes down. Horn ain't a jasper takes to interruptions well."

"Hell with his disposition. I've rode two horses in the ground getting here and working on the third one."

"Your life." The bartender shrugged, unconcerned.

Slocum boarded the steep, narrow staircase. His boot soles ground fresh grit into the worn wood on each flight.

At the top he opened the door to the narrow dark hallway. He could hear a woman down on the theater floor singing. In the loft, the girls could pull the drapes for privacy from the crowd downstairs, leaving a narrow room to ply their trade in. *Wide enough for one—deep enough for two* best described the arrangement.

In the dimly lighted shallow passageway, Slocum moved sideways. The grunting coming from the first room left no doubt that the parties inside were engaged. In room two a man and woman were whispering in an argument about "getting it up." Slocum listened at the third thin door. Nothing.

He cracked the door slowly open. In the dim light from the drapes he could make out Horn's thin bare butt sticking up. He was sprawled over a naked woman lying on her back, and both looked passed out. The woman's strong perfume nearly gagged Slocum.

Slocum nudged him with his boot. "Get up, Horn, we got business."

"Business?" Horn mumbled, not moving.

The woman's eyes flew open and she screamed. Horn's hand quickly silenced her. "You come to kill me or tell me I just won a jackpot? It better be good to disturb me at a time like this."

"Neither. Geronimo wants you to meet him. He's giving himself up to Crook."

"Jesus, man! Why didn't you say so." In a flash, Horn was on his feet dressing. His female companion crawfished up to a sitting position using the thin blanket to hide her nudity as Horn stumbled around dressing in the close quarters.

"Hell, honey, he's seen more hide than you've got showing."

"You coming back?" she asked, ignoring his comments.

"Sure, darling, but I got army business to tend to right now. But you keep that sweet ass warm for me while I'm away, won't you?"

She rose to her feet, clutching the blanket as well as

eyeing Slocum with distrust for not having the decency to step out of the narrow room.

"I will. You be real careful, baby," she said, trying to get Tom's attention.

He finally quickly kissed her on the puckered mouth, then went back to stomping on his boots. He found his hat on the floor and slapped it on his head; then he hugged her hard and the blanket fell away as she clung to him and they kissed again.

Her perfume by then had overpowered Slocum, and he stepped back into the hallway. No way to escape it. On his empty belly, the scent was too much.

"You look done in," Horn said, emerging and buckling on his gunbelt.

"I rode up from Paso the past twenty-four hours."

"Long damn ways."

"I wanted to find you because you have barely got over a week to set up the deal."

"So," Horn said when they reached the top of the stairs. "The old desert fox wants to come back?"

Slocum ambled down the stairs with a nod in reply to Horn. "He says he will for you or Gatewood. But when I told him the lieutenant was gone, he asked for you."

"By Gawd, I better ride up and see Crook at Fort Bowie, huh?"

"He said he would be at Skull Canyon in ten days if you will meet them there ahead of time, and then you can bring along General Crook."

"Let's go up to Nellie Cashman's and get us a meal before we do anything else." Horn took off his hat and scratched his too-long hair. "I can't think on an empty stomach."

"Good idea. What's wrong?"

"I can't recall where in the hell I left my damn horse." Horn searched around among the bunch hitched in front. "I don't see him."

"I'll get mine," Slocum said. "Maybe you'll recall where you left yours on the way."

22

The stage rocked from side to side. Dust swirled through with little respect for the pair that shared the coach with three men: two drummers in brown suits and a nice-looking engineer from the Lucky Lady Mine.

"Martin McCurdy," the engineer introduced himself removing his hat for her.

"Lucia Sallisar," she said. "Pleased to meet you, sir."

"Robins," the red-faced drummer in the middle said. "Hide Robins, I represent the firm of Hayes and Cormack. Selling mining equipment is my line of work."

"Torg Swenson of Minnesota. I sell the ladies' apparel for my company."

"Nice to meet all of you. This is my ranch foreman, John Shade," she said, indicating Slocum. He raised the brim of his hat, looked at the three, and let it drop down so he could go back to sleep.

He'd introduced her as his wife to Pershing, so he guessed her introducing him as her ranch foreman was suitable for a traveling companion. But she'd said it as if she didn't want anymore association other than a working one with him. Maybe she liked the engineer McCurdy; he looked like a suitable capture. The two drummers were just excited to have an attractive woman to talk to.

"Where is your ranch?" McCurdy asked her.

160

"In Mexico near the small village of Santa Cristo," she said.

"You must have a hacienda there."

"Yes, it is my family's estate."

"I have been to Mexico, but never that region. Perhaps someday I will be in the area," McCurdy said.

"Do drop in, sir," she said, "when you are in the area of the hacienda."

And she was the one who said she hated to act like a society lady, Slocum mused under his hat. Why, to listen to her was worse than some dowager at a society ball. If the engineer ever went down there, she would probably be gone, or her father would deny she was real and tell him he had been hoaxed by a fraud. There had to be some way he could teach Sallisar a lesson. Hell, he wasn't God and couldn't cure all the ills in the world; finding a suitable mate for her would be enough. Forget the stupid bastard.

Lucia did look breathtakingly handsome in the new blue dress and box hat from the Tombstone milliner. It would be the perfect outfit to find a man with in Tucson. He hoped to get her set up and be on his own way in a week.

McCurdy and the girl found plenty to talk about. The depressed silver prices, the dry weather, and the effect on cattle prices. By late afternoon the stage swung into Tucson and the two stood talking while her "foreman" arranged for their luggage to be sent to the Congress Hotel.

"Martin says he is very interested in searching the Madres for mineral deposits. I told him you were a very good guide."

"Maybe when the Apaches surrender," he said, looking for a carriage to take them to the hotel. "I'll go back."

"Ha, that looks like a long time, sir." McCurdy shook his head. "I meant in my lifetime."

"It may be sooner than you think."

She parted with McCurdy with some effort when Slocum found a carriage to take the two of them to their hotel.

"Interesting man," Slocum said once they were alone. "Is he married?"

"How should I know?"

"That's your business here, to know if they are single or married. If he's married, don't waste your time on him."

"You sound like this is a bull-buying expedition."

"Same thing," he said.

She put her slender hand on his leg familiarly. "If I get married to someone will you come around and visit?"

"Not likely."

She wrinkled her nose at him as if she was mad at his answer, and then folded her arms in a pout.

"No need to be mad," he said. "We are here on business and it is your future we're working on."

"Maybe we should go to El Paso."

"You don't like married life, then you can do that. But don't make up your mind."

She shook her head. "I hope you are right."

"Trust me."

She moved her hand deftly up his leg and gave him a private dig. "I will." Then she straightened up ladylike as they reached the hotel.

Slocum stood back with a drink in his hand on the edge of the ballroom. He watched the dark-haired young man swirl Lucia Sallisar across the floor. Lorenzo Montez was his name—a hacienda owner's son that she had met years before. He acted thunderstruck enough to be the perfect victim that Slocum had hoped for.

She stopped to speak to Slocum, out of breath, with excitement dancing in her eyes. "He wants to meet my father. What shall I tell him?"

"Does he want you or your riches?"

"I don't know," she said in a loud whisper.

"Handle it like that."

Her dark eyes cut around as she was displeased with his reply. "He wonders too why I have no chaperone?"

"You might ought to wait for a gringo that is not so smart about such things."

She looked at the ceiling for help. "You are no help." With that she moved away to the buffet on the long table.

Slocum watched her for a long while before he interested himself in viewing a tall redhead. Was she married? She looked like fun, with deep cleavage that rose and fell when she moved, her figure looking ample enough to be a bedful of pleasure under a man.

"Mr. Slocum?"

He turned to face the engineer, McCurdy. It was their first meeting since the stage.

"Yes?"

"What is she doing here?" The man furrowed his brow in a scowl of distrust.

"Pardon?"

"In the first place, hacienda owners don't allow their single daughters to run around without a chaperone or their mother and in the company of a foreman—did she say?"

"You have honest intentions toward her?"

The man frowned. "I like her—yes, in fact I do."

"You aren't married?"

"No, and I've never been. Are you some relation to her?" Anger blackened McCurdy's face as they stood at the edge of the ballroom. The orchestra began to play again.

It was time to take a chance and be honest with the man. "She eloped to marry a young man beneath her station. He became afraid and deserted her when the padre would not marry them. Then she was kidnapped. I found her and returned her to her parents, not knowing her father's intentions to lock her up. I took her from the convent at her request. Do you know enough now?"

"Exactly," he said, and started across the floor for her and the boy. In a moment, Slocum saw the tall man with blond sideburns whirling the blue dress around the floor.

"Who is he?" Montez demanded of Slocum.

"I think his name is McCurdy, an engineer from Tombstone," he said.

"Who is this woman? She says she has no fortune, yet she is the only daughter of Don Sallisar?"

"I think he has cut her out of his will."

The flush-faced youth clenched his fists at his side. "And

why are you here with her?'' His face was dangerously close to Slocum's.

"Because like you I love her.''

"Huh?''

"You would never understand. I think you lost, amigo,'' Slocum said as he watched the dancing pair laugh, light-footed, weaving in great circles through the other couples as if they were the only ones.

"Lost what?''

"I think Martin McCurdy is going to nose you right out.''

"I will challenge him to a duel.''

"And get killed?'' Slocum asked.

The youth shook his head as if he had considered something different. "Then I shall go get drunk.''

Slocum clapped him on the shoulder. "A damn sight better idea.''

It was long past midnight when the soft knock on his door brought him up to a sitting position.

"Open up,'' she whispered.

He unlocked the door with the key and looked both ways up and down the corridor as she swept by him with her skirts in hand. The bed protested as she bounced in the center of it.

"It worked!'' she gushed. "No need for a lamp. I had to come tell you. McCurdy and I are going to be married in the morning. And you know he doesn't care a thing about my past.''

"You told him?''

"Yes,'' she said. "Come here. I have to hug somcone and I owe you so much.''

"You had better save yourself for the big honeymoon,'' he said, looking at the slow dray passing under the street lamp below the room.

"It will be my last chance to be with you. Slocum, come here.'' She tugged on his arm.

He shook his head, but let himself be drawn down to the bed.

"Undo my dress so it doesn't get all wrinkled, please," she requested, turning her back to him. "It won't take you long to do that."

Sun bathed the room the next morning. He had decided not to attend her wedding. He combed his hair back seated on the edge of the bed, recalling the tenderness of their final parting. He would head back to see the witch and his friends at Paso. Perhaps if there had been time, Geronimo would have showed him where gold came from the mountains.

He took breakfast in the hotel and then paid the bill for their rooms. All told, he was down to thirty dollars. Enough to get a one-way coach fare to Tombstone, hitch a ride over to the fort, pay the week's livery bill, and ride south with his horses. Goldfarb had given them and the saddles to him, but he needed to return them—the gift was too generous.

He stepped onto the sidewalk as the paperboy rushed up. "Geronimo breaks the peace! Mister, you want to read about it?"

He took the paper and absently paid the boy.

Ft. Huacuhua, Arizona Territory—Apaches quit peace talks and return to mountains in Mexico. While the command of General Crook and the Pacific command has not issued an official statement on the status of the talks, this reporter has learned that legendary chief of the Chiricahua Apaches, Geronimo, and his band of hostiles met with Crook recently below the U.S.-Mexico border in a much-heralded end to the costly, bloody war. Terms of the peace with the Apaches were not disclosed, but most experts expected the President of the United States to turn these heartless killers over to civilian authorities for trial of the numerous charges of bloody massacres, rape, and pillage of citizens on both sides of the border. However, after numerous meetings at a remote

location, the Apaches obviously became dissat-
isfied and took the opportunity to withdraw into the
Sierra Madre Mountains without a clue, not only
leaving General George Crook looking red-faced
and empty-handed, but with demands for his res-
ignation flooding the military commands.

Border communities are ordering local militias
to full arms. The rabid red men are on the move
again. More news of their atrocities and death of
innocent citizens will no doubt soon blood-soak
the newspapers in the Southwest.

Slocum hurried to catch the stage. He knew by this time
Lucia must be looking around for him at the office of the
justice of the peace. But they were adults and didn't need
his consent; besides, he felt certain his personal losses were
great enough to avoid another parting with her.

Damn, Crook and Tom had missed closing the deal with
Geronimo. No way to tell what had gone wrong—they
would certainly have a military shakeup after all this. Pa-
pers and politicians could crucify the general—Nantan Lupan was the Apaches' last friend in high places. The desert
fox might have outsmarted himself, with Mexicans and the
U.S. both after him. He might do as Natise said—*die in
those mountains.*

Slocum climbed on the stage. In a few hours McCurdy
would claim his new bride. He hoped she could live with
one man. No matter, he was Mexico-bound and Lucia Sallisar was a McCurdy. He sat back in the front seat and
closed his eyes to shut out a memory of her passion. Gawdamn!

In Tombstone, he asked about Tom Horn, but no one had
seen him in several days. So he caught a ride to the fort,
paid for his horses' stay, saddled them and made a lead line
from halter to saddlehorn.

"You've got enough gawdamn horses and saddles to
start your own stables," the old hustler commended; then

he punctuated his speech with a squirt of black tobacco juice into the dust.

"I may do that," Slocum said. Nosey old bastard, none of his business how many horses Slocum kept.

"Don't get your ass throwed over your shoulder," the old man said, and stalked off mumbling about soreheads in the world.

Slocum had mounted up when he noticed a familiar black horse coming down the street. It was Jack Pershing, Lieutenant, U.S. Tenth Cavalry.

"Guess you really tried to bring those hostiles in, Mr. Slocum." Jack grinned. "I heard how you set it up."

Slocum shook his head to dismiss the praise.

"Where's the wife?" Pershing asked looking at all the saddle horses as if expecting her to appear.

"Actually, she was my ward. I told you that to save explaining a lot."

"You mean she wasn't your wife?" Pershing squinted hard at him in disbelief. "She was the most handsome woman I have ever seen. If I'd known that—why I'd—"

"She wasn't my wife and yes, she was very pretty. She married a man called McCurdy today."

"You mean the engineer up at the Lucky Lady mine? Why, I know him. How did he meet her?" the young officer demanded. "I saw her before he did."

"Sorry, Lieutenant," he said, and turned his horse to leave.

"I am too."

"Good luck, Pershing. Maybe you'll find another girl that pretty someday."

"Yes sir."

Slocum crossed the south pass and took his time returning. Satisfied the Apaches were further south, he bathed in the Blanco with his guns close by, then rode on to Santa Cristo.

After dark, he left his horse with a farmer and came on foot through the wall by the stables' outlet under the cover of darkness. He rapped on Estrallia's back door softly. She came wrapping herself, and blinked in disbelief at him.

"I have company," she whispered, and tossed her head.

"Sorry," he said, and started to leave. She came outside, belting the robe she wore. Then she parted the long hair in her face and moved it back.

"You look thin," she said as she stood barefoot in the alley.

"I didn't know." He indicated the casa with head toss. "He is just a friend."

"No matter. I will ride on. Another day I will return."

She shook her head. "I know you are kind to say such things, but you won't return, will you?"

"Oh, someday."

"God, be with you," she said, and turned on her heel to go back inside.

He found the horses without waking a soul and re-saddled them; then he left the farmer a small pouch of change on a string tied to the corral gate. In the saddle, he gave a wave with his hand toward the dark *jacale* where the man, his short, part-Indian wife, and a half-dozen children slept.

"Sleep tight, amigo, and put your hand on her rump to check she is still there. You are lucky for you have a woman—all mine are gone," he said softly to the bay horse that he rode.

23

The smoke warned him something was wrong. Beyond the low foothill range he could see the black cloud pillowing skyward. He dismounted and switched bridles to the roan, knowing the other horses would follow if he turned them loose. A large knot churned in his empty belly—there were bad things happening at Paeo. He spurred the roan into a run. No time to waste, but he felt certain he was too late—damn, he had warned Goldfarb.

The first *jacale* he rode up to was burned out. Bodies of dead children lay in the dust as he paused, nauseated at the sight. A woman's body without clothing lay under the edge of the pulled-down remada. Her bare brown legs coated in dust were spread unnaturally wide where they stuck out.

Forcing down the bile rising in his throat, he pushed the roan on, past more smouldering ruins of farmers' huts and houses. Bodies, young and old, were strewn about, reminding him of when lightning had killed three hundred steers a decade before on a cattle drive he had made to Wichita.

He saw the source of the black smoke coming from the mercantile ahead. The cantina and small shops were nearly burned out across the street when he drew his horse up and slid off with his gun in hand.

Where were the butchers? Were they red or white. The earth was not big enough for them to hide in. He rushed across the street past several corpses—was no one alive? Inside the door, he saw the great pink body hung by its thumbs from ropes tied up high on the second floor, head limp on its chest. Goldfarb was dead.

He'd been mutilated by his tormentors, and the strain and terror were still etched on the man's face. Slocum climbed on the counter, drew out his knife, and slashed the ropes to allow the body to tumble to the floor.

He was weary with his findings, and his eyes smarted from the smoke as he knelt beside the corpse, which he covered with a blanket. "Sorry, old friend. I should have stayed." He rose wearily, and then with leaden boots he started up the stairs. Where was Ruby?

Nothing had escaped the savagry of the raiders. They had looted every shelf, and what they had not taken was smashed and spilled in wanton fashion on the floor. Sacks of flour poured everywhere like snow, with rice and beans underfoot like drifts. Drunken madmen had been there.

He looked in the room where he usually slept. The bedding was shredded and the drapes jerked down. In the next room he was not ready for the sight. Ruby huddled naked on the floor in the corner. She hugged a remaining drape, her face bruised purple, and at the sight of him, she began to scream.

He went to her. "It's me, Slocum." She drew away at his touch and screamed louder.

"I am here to help you, Ruby, please?"

She twisted trying to escape him—nothing he could say could stop her fear or shut down the horror inside her. Finally, despite her cries, he lifted her protesting form and rose looking for a suitable bed to put her upon. The screams she made had ceased to bother him; he wanted her comfortable.

"Who did this?" he asked her over and over. He kicked things out of his way—finally she was reduced to sobbing and clinging to him. He finally spotted an unturned cot and laid her gently down. "Who did this?"

"McVain—"

The name slapped him like the force of a great ocean

wave. Rage ripped out of his vocal cords; the cry for revenge reverberated up the canyons and bounced off the Madre slopes. He beat his fists on the wall and kicked the side of the room until the plaster dust rose in clouds and cut off his wind. Finally he fell on his knees and prayed for the strength to find this killer of men, women, and children and to let justice prevail.

Then he tasted the salt of his own tears and buried his face in his sleeves.

In a while, he discovered she was sleeping, drawn in a ball like a baby in a womb. A whimpering sleep that made her shoulders shake and moans escaped her lips. He covered her with rags of blankets. Resting would cure some of her pain; nothing would ever cure all of it.

Were there others alive? He must learn if there were survivors. With dread in his heart he started down the hallway.

He came out the door of the store with his pistol drawn. Then he saw them; they were bewildered-looking with bandages and on makeshift crutches. Men, women, and children who had survived.

Finally two younger men carried an older one out in the open before the store. At first Slocum did not recognize the man they sat before him, his face purple, his eyes slits under the bruises.

"Sanchez, is that you?"

"*Sí*, amigo, I am glad to see you." The man smiled in pain, then reached up and Slocum took his hand. "We are all glad to see you."

"When did they attack?"

"Yesterday. They came in and started killing, raping, scalping, and shooting everything. Little children—"

"I saw that, amigo. They went back in the mountains?"

"*Sí*."

"I will go after them."

"But what can one man do?"

"I don't know, but I'll do something."

"Don't be foolish," Sanchez protested. "They will only kill you."

"Take care of Ruby, Sanchez, she will need a woman."

"We will, but señor, you can't go by yourself against such butchers."

Slocum viewed the dark slopes of the towering Madres and wet his cracked lips. Somehow, some way, he would find these butchers and exact his own revenge on them. They did not deserve to live another day—not a one of them. He shut his lids to cut out the grimy scene and the acrid smoke that burnt his eyes.

24

"Why should we help you?" Natise demanded.

"The scalpers have attacked you and your people. He is your enemy." Slocum twisted the stick in his hand, gouging at the loose dirt and tracing the point in the cracks in the hard-baked *caliche* in front of where he sat cross-legged in the circle of Apache men.

"But there are many guns in his camp."

Slocum rose to his feet as if ready to leave. "I thought the Apache feared no man. Have I come to a camp of women?"

"Sit," Natise ordered. "If these killers of women and young boys were so easy to kill, we would have done it moons ago."

Slocum eased back to the ground and re-crossed his legs. Those were the first encouraging words from Natise since he'd began to ask for his assistance in ridding the world of the cutthroat scalpers.

"Did you ask Geronimo to help?" Natise asked.

"Not yet."

"Why not?"

"Because I decided to start with you. You are the head of the Chiricahuas."

Natise shook his head in somber denial. "They go with whom they wish."

"Still, if I can say to Geronimo that Natise, the chief of these people, is ready to ride against the scalpers, can he say no?"

"He can and probably will."

"No, he will come in and we will all ride together after these butchers of children."

"I hear there is bad blood between you and Tomatoes." Natise's eyes formed narrow slits as he waited for an answer.

"Tomatoes was jilted by a white woman. He thinks I did that to him."

"Did you?"

"No, he was too greedy and wanted two wives. She wanted to be the only one."

"Will you ask him to join us?"

"Yes."

Natise grinned. "I like you, Slocum. You faced that big bear Tomatoes as if you had no fear of him that day when we traded with you and he came looking for her."

The others chuckled and agreed with head bobs about his feat of being brave in the face of such anger.

"Worse than that, the woman—she was in his camp and Tomatoes never knew it," an old man said, the same one who had spoken to him in the store. They laughed again and then grinned at his antics.

"She did not wish to share his blankets with another woman." Slocum added.

"Do you know a good witch?" Natise asked.

"Why?"

"We need a good one to tell us what time to make this attack and our medicine man is dead."

"I know one. But I will have to find the scalpers' camp first, then go to Geronimo, Tomatoes—"

Natise was shaking his head back and forth. Finally he spoke. "The scalpers are camped a day's ride from here. We know where they sleep. You go learn from this witch what is the best time we should attack. I will tell Geronimo and Tomatoes about the plans and to be ready."

"Good," Slocum said, hardly able to believe he had convinced Natise to help him end the scalpers' rein of terror.

He accepted the pottery cup from the squaw who kneeled beside him. She smiled for him as she rose; he wondered if he knew her from the stomp dances of years gone by. Probably not, for she hardly looked older than in her late teens.

"Let us drink the whiskey of the white men and forget our homelands lost," Natise said, and raised his cup. The other men, as if on signal, spoke in guttural Apache and lifted their vessels in salute.

The liquor was raw and tainted with enough red pepper to scald Slocum's tongue and throat going down. He actually liked their pulpy *tiswain* better than the firewater, but he supposed the women had no time on the run to grub out the century plant roots, bake and then ferment them.

The same woman returned, squatted before him, and served him the skinned hind quarter of a ground squirrel, still steaming hot from the boiling pot. The meat was sweet in his mouth, and once or twice he discouraged his own thoughts that his meal might be a large bush rat.

He knew Apaches boiled them whole and then completed butchering the carcass before serving them. Despite his misgivings, he could hardly deny the handsome smiling face who had situated herself before him and held the plate to serve him.

"What is your name?" he asked.

"Melon," she said, and her eyes danced with excitement that he asked.

"Slo-cum," he said.

She nodded that she knew his name. "You want to dance?" she asked, her gaze not leaving him.

She squatted on her boot toes not three feet from him, and if he didn't know for certain, he suspected she had edged closer as they talked. Her slender nose had been broken for some time, for a small hump appeared halfway down the bridge. He could smell her sweet musk even with his sense dulled by the powerful whiskey. He speculated how mouth-watering her skin would taste.

Then someone dropped beside him. In his knee-high

boots, the intruder squatted to Slocum's right. Then he heard Natise's voice in his ear.

"There will be times later for you to make moves in Melon. She can wait. Now you must go speak to this witch." Natise took a drink from his cup. Then he made an "ah" sound, clearing his throat. "Is this witch you go to see a good one?"

Still staring into the deep pools of brown that reflected his own desires, he nodded yes. "A helluva good one."

"Good, you ride for her and hurry back."

He reached Santa Cristo by sundown, and made his way carefully inside the livery stable and up the alleyway. He paused to check that no one had observed his entry. He knocked softly. No answer. He waited—was she gone on a call to aid the sick or helping someone birth a baby somewhere?

What should he do? The evening was still early; perhaps she was not far away doctoring someone. He took a seat and put his back to the plastered wall. In a few minutes he dozed, and after a while the sounds of someone inside her house awoke him. The moon was coming up, so he knew he had slept some time.

His ear to the thin door, he listened for the sound of more than one person inside the room. Only one footfall could he hear as that person stoked the fire and clanked cooking pots. Quietly, he undid the door and eased inside the back room. On his tiptoes, he moved carefully to the doorway, then spotted a weatherbeaten Stetson on the table. His heart stopped. He knew that hat.

"Damn, if I wasn't starved as a grizzly bear we'd just go to bed right now," Tom Horn said aloud.

"And what would I eat?" Slocum demanded as both of them whirled around wide-eyed at his entrance.

"What the hell are you doing here?" Tom asked. He gave Estrallia a peeved look and then scowled at Slocum.

"I come to get some information from Estrallia and now to recruit you. And tell me why in the hell Geronimo ran off from Crook and you all?"

"I think he got spooked by some witch predicting some bad end. See, they all got drunk on this damn Mexican's whiskey that night. He sold them a mule-load of it for near nothing. The plan I figured out was them Mexicans wanted the Chiricahuas drunk and then they planned to ambush the whole bunch of them before Crook could take them back. But Crook got wind of something and some of the scouts spooked off the ambushers. But by then Geronimo was nervous about the deal, and they all fled. Shit-fire, it was all a big damn mistake. Hell, I hated it for Crook's sake. He was the only friend them people ever had in the military."

"I've got a plan." Slocum turned to Estrallia. "When would be the best time I could attack my enemies?"

"Which ones?"

"McVain."

He heard Tom suck in wind and gasp and bolt upright in his chair. "The damn scalpers. You plan to take on that bunch that gunned down Captain Crawford?"

"I figured you'd want to help." He turned back to look at her.

"When the rain comes down the canyon," she said, then nodded thoughtfully over her words. "I don't know when, but I know it will work when the rain comes down the canyon."

"Gal, that don't make a lot of sense. Rain in the canyon? Hell, that's maybe weeks from now. The way it rains around here it could mean next year."

"No, it will rain soon in the mountains."

"Good enough. You ready to ride?" Slocum asked Horn.

"God sake, man, let me eat something anyway. You've upset all my other plans so far this evening."

"Where's your horse?"

"Tied up out front," Tom said, and then they both laughed again about their search all over Tombstone the night when Tom forgot where he'd hitched his horse. After hours of looking all over, they'd found it right across the street from the Bird Cage where they had been in the first place.

"Who's in on this deal?" Tom asked.

"You, me, and the Chiricahuas."

Tom nodded his approval as he dipped some of the sauce out of a bowl she'd set before him onto a fresh tortilla.

"Damn, Estrallia, why don't you marry one of the two of us?" Tom asked.

She looked at them mildly. "And have to choose between two such *grande* hombres? No, I would rather have both of you come to see me every ten years or so."

"Ten years?" Tom squeaked like pig caught under a gate. "That ain't so."

"Yes, it is. You and Slocum only ride this way when you have no credit with *putas,* I think."

Both men looked at each other and shook their heads in disappointment.

"How could you believe such a thing?" Tom asked.

"Slocum rode up here a few months ago. You"—she pointed at Tom—"have not been to my casa in over a year. Yes, you come whenever your gun gets hard, but I would not be married to such men who only needs a woman every once in a long while."

Tom wiped his mouth on his sleeve and gave her a rueful look. "I daresay, partner, the way she talks about the pair of us . . ."

"She won't be home anyway if she was married. She gets called away all the time to cure the sick," Slocum said.

Estrallia privately frowned at him, then grinned. "See there! I am no good as a wife either. No one should marry me."

"We'll talk more about it when we come back," Tom said with a tortilla in one hand as he filled it with her spicy meat and bean sauce and stood straddling the chair. "We've got scalpers to eliminate."

"You will be careful?" She looked at both of them.

"We always are," Tom said, and kissed her quickly.

Slocum nodded in agreement. "I'll meet you on the road. My horse is out back."

"Darling, darling . . ." Horn's words to her trailed off as Slocum slipped out through the back door into the inky night. *Rain comes down the canyon*—he would have to tell Natise the sign she had given him. There were plenty of things left to do. He glanced at the star struck sky—they would need to be certain of surprise to take McVain's camp.

He untied the reins from the mesquite tree and bounded into the saddle. Next he had to meet Tom Horn.

25

Slocum and Horn crossed the Devil's Crossing under the spears of morning gold that shot over the peaks above them. Grateful to be across, both mounts shook hard when the two men dismounted and drained their bladders.

"What's a man going to do when these renegades finally hang up their war stuff?" Tom asked, preparing to remount.

"Get a job in town, I guess, barkeep or run a store."

"Hell, Slocum, I can't count past ten the same way three times in row."

"Maybe become a lawman. Work for one of them detective agencies."

"I guess I'll just drift around till I find something."

"These Injun wars are about all over, aren't they?" Slocum mounted his horse.

"They ain't enough left to have war over—a handful of Chiricahuas. They got buffalo soldiers watching every water hole and stinking sink north of the border. Just a matter of time. They're replacing Crook with Miles and he don't know his ass for the hole in the ground about this bunch. But he gets enough troops down here he may learn how to kill a mouse with twenty .50-caliber Sharps."

"Only one thing worries me," Slocum said as they remounted.

"What's that?"

"That those damn Apaches remember who you are and why I'm coming back to their camp."

"Stands to reason, partner." Tom removed his high-crown hat and tied his red neckerchief around the crown. Holding it out, he examined his work. "There, that ought to help some."

Late afternoon they rode up the canyon where they expected to find Natise's camp. The brush was head-high along the dry watercourse, and both men had taken repeated turns twisting in the saddle to look for any unseen enemy.

"There he is," Slocum said as the armed figure drove his horse into plain sight. The rider was Geronimo and except for breechcloth and a blue bandanna, he was naked. His bare skin shone in the sun as he balanced the rifle on his knee.

"Took you a long time," Geronimo said.

Natise pushed his horse out in the pathway. "What do you hear from your witch?"

"She said to attack when the rain comes down the canyon."

Natise nodded and pointed at the sky for everyone to listen. Slocum looked at Tom. Was that distant thunder?

"We must ride," Natise shouted, and the hills became alive with riders hidden in the timber up the steep slope. At his words, the small chief sent his pony scrambling up the steep face of the mountain.

"He say where they were at?" Tom asked.

"Nope, let's find out!" Slocum gave the gray his head, and he began to dig uphill in great cat-hops.

Natise took a course southwest. By his own count, Slocum figured there were two dozen riders, from boys in their teens to warriors, all on good horses and stripped to the skin for the fight, like the scouts always wanted to do when it looked like they would tangle with the hostiles. An Apache just fought better naked.

"How much further to their camp?" Tom asked as they tore through some tall open timber.

"Beats me. I've never been to this one."

The sky broke open from a dark cloud moving fast across

the range. Natise reined up as the two white men drew out their slickers.

"Their camp is ahead," Natise said. "They think they can ride out the other end, but Tomatoes's band is there."

"There is a big man in that camp who helped me warn Geronimo when they closed in on his camp. I would save him if I may."

Natise agreed and looked around as heads nodded. The vote was yes. But Slocum would be the one who had to retrieve his friend Meyers—if he was still there with the scalpers.

Raindrops beat on Slocum's slicker. Thunder pealed across the Madres like a great kettle drum. The raid began, and riders began to spread out into the trees without command. Apaches knew how to launch an attack.

"You ever fought on their side before?" Tom asked.

"Nope."

"First time I went in a whorehouse, this big old gal asked me the same thing. And she said, we all had to do it first once anyway." His Colt drawn, he checked his horse and grinned at Slocum.

"Let's go help them!"

Gunshots began to fill the air. The wind and rain grew more intense and the war cries of the Chiricahuas grew louder—the cursing of men, wounded horses screaming. Many of the scalpers were riding for their lives; they broke from the ring and fled into the forest.

Slocum searched for Meyers, but saw no sign of the man. He looked at the dead and wounded lying on the muddy ground. More rain swept through trees and naked warriors searched the goods. The attack was over! Several scalpers had managed to get away. Perhaps his friend had gotten away. A handful lay dead.

"McVain has escaped," Natise said, riding up.

"You got his tracks?" Tom asked.

"They go north."

"I owe that bastard," Horn said, "for Captain Crawford and the rest. Give us two good trackers. We'll get him," he said to Natise, and indicated Slocum with his thumb.

"You can have those boys," the chief said, and waved the pair over. "Go with these men and help them find the man who wears dresses. The killer of women and children."

Both boys nodded and rushed off for their horses. Tom reached out to shake Natise's hand. The man did not offer his.

Tom frowned as he sat back up in the saddle. "Miles will hound you to the ends of these mountains, amigo."

"Tell him to come, I will die here," Natise said.

"We better ride," Slocum said to Tom, afraid they might wear out what little welcome they had with the Apaches anyway.

Horn agreed with a nod, but still looked confused at Natise's determination. Slocum and Horn joined the two scouts; they hurried northward. The rain had quit, but the gusts of winds were sharp. The youths pointed out that McVain had circled around missing Tomatoes's trap. Both Slocum and Tom were forced to hurry their horses to keep up with the boys who studied the trail carefully, then rode like wild men.

When it was dark, they made a dry camp and chewed on some year-old jerky Tom had in his saddlebags for their supper. Determined to sleep a few hours, Slocum wondered how the two Apaches would keep from freezing with simply shirts and loincloths for warmth.

When they rode out of the mountains the next morning, McVain's direction was so obvious, north, that they sent the boys back to their bands.

At noontime, they rode up on a goat herder's camp in the hills.

"You watch things out here." Slocum dismounted when no one answered his greeting. Goats crowded around him.

He stuck his head inside the open door and saw a yearling on top of the table bleating and looking down in the face of a dead man. His throat had been slashed and he lay in a pool of blood.

Slocum swallowed hard and went back outside. "Too late to help the man," he said, and remounted his horse.

"Makes another life he owes for," Tom said, "but there are too many to count."

"He's avoiding the fort, isn't he?" Slocum asked after considering the direction McVain was headed.

"He's going either for the train depot at Fairbanks or for Tombstone."

"I'll bet he has a suitcase full of blood money and he's heading out of the country."

"Let's ride as fast as we can and get to Fairbanks. He's there, we might be able to stop him before he gets away." Tom whipped his pony into a run and Slocum was right after him. They crossed the sun-cured bunchgrass slapping at their boot toes, the green line of the San Pedro river drawing closer when Slocum saw the trail of black smoke. A train was coming up from Nogales. They'd have to hurry.

"I see it," Tom shouted with a wary shake of his head. They forced their horses to go faster. "This way is shorter."

They reined up nearly a quarter mile from the station, cut off by a short bluff. Damn. Slocum dropped his gaze to the ground. There was no way to stop him now. They could never get around and down there in time. The approaching train was coming up the valley with its whistle wailing, the trailing smoke above the cottonwood tops.

Slocum could even make out the red plaid dress as he pounded his saddle. About that moment, Tom rounded his horse, raising the ears on the single-shot Sharps rifle's sights.

"That's him on the platform, ain't it?" Tom asked.

"It damn sure is."

Tom drew the rifle to his shoulder and dropped his face down on the cheek piece, and the great gun belched a bullet and cloud of smoke. The sound of the charge carried down the San Pedro waterway. Folks at the Lucky Lady Mine in Tombstone heard the echo. Lt. Jack Pershing of the Tenth noticed the gun report while working with a detail of his men on a waterworks for the fort on the side of the Huachuca Mountains high in the south.

Slocum watched the man's arms fly skyward as he was

hit hard, and then as if jerked from the train platform by some great force, McVain disappeared backward as the steam engine and passenger cars arrived like a stage curtain at the Fairbank's station and closed off Slocum's view.

"Guess I need to stash this old gun with a Mexican gal that I know. Folks will be asking lots of questions about who owns a .50-caliber. After that, I'm treating you to the best meal and one of the greatest whores in Tombstone," Tom said, jamming the gun into the scabbard and coming around to mount up. "That shot was for Captain Crawford, wasn't it?"

"And a lot of others. I may do the buying," Slocum said, watching the distant crowd like ants swarming around the stalled train. "For an old friend of mine." He wondered how Ruby was doing—he would certainly miss that big husband of hers.

October, 1886. Slocum was dealing faro in Trinidad, Colorado, at Molly Moore's saloon. He was taking a break when someone rushed in with a newspaper fresh off the train.

"They've got pictures of General Miles and Geronimo surrendering."

"Here, give that to me," he said. Sure enough, on the front page there was a picture of Geronimo, and with him Natise, Tomatoes, and the others—Lt. Gatewood, General Miles, and with his cowboy hat half cocked on his head, Tom Horn, grinning like the cat that ate the canary in their midst.

Slocum handed the newspaper back to the man, then turned and ordered a double shot of good whiskey. He downed it in memory of his late friend Goldfarb and for Lucia, Estrallia, and Ruby. The Chiricahuas' days were over. Someday he would go back and bathe in the Rio Blanco again. Sometime—but not soon.